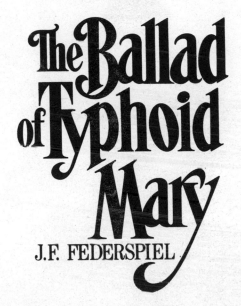

The Ballad of Typhoid Mary

J.F. FEDERSPIEL

ILLUSTRATIONS BY LARRY SCHWINGER
TRANSLATED BY JOEL AGEE

BALLANTINE BOOKS • NEW YORK

Library of Congress Catalog Card Number: 83-8938

ISBN 0-345-31967-2

This edition published by arrangement with E. P. Dutton, Inc.

Excerpts from *The Curious Career of Typhoid Mary* by George A. Soper,
M.D., reprinted by permission from *The Bulletin* of the New York Acad-
emy of Medicine, October 1939.

Manufactured in the United States of America

First Ballantine Books Edition: February 1985

For Lea

Life is strange and the world is bad.

THOMAS WOLFE

In the early morning hours of January 11, 1868, a ship emerged from the whirling snow outside New York Harbor and remained unnoticed by the harbor authorities until after she had violated the three-mile limit. But that was not only due to the twilight and to the snow obstructing the view across the blackish waters—there was something amiss: nothing had awakened the sleepy coast guard, no shouts of joy, such as could usually be heard from immigrant ships arriving from Europe. An officer named Remigius Farrell reported to the immigration authorities: "It was like looking at a cutout in silhouette. The sails were torn to shreds, the mast was broken. We were still fifty feet away when the wind brought the combined stench of feces and dead bodies. Almost all immigrant ships stink, but this was unbearable."

The *Leibnitz*—that was the name of this wreck which had once been a sailing ship—had been excellently built in Boston, and was originally intended for trade with China; later it was acquired by the Sloman's Hamburg Line, a shipping company which, until then, could boast of a flawless reputation. The *Leibnitz* had left Hamburg on November 2, 1867; under Captain H. F. Bornholm. She had been forced to lie at anchor outside Cuxhaven for several days, due to unfavorable winds. Therefore, the captain decided upon the southern route (via Madeira) to New York, along latitudes that would subject the passengers to temperatures of up to ninety-four degrees Fahrenheit. Many of them came from Mecklenburg and wanted to settle as farmers in Wisconsin; others came from Prussia, and a few from southern Germany and from Switzerland.

The passage across the Atlantic must have been infernal. Anything that took up space had been removed so that 544 passengers could be loaded aboard, literally like cargo. Anyone trying to imagine the prospect of overpopulation in our twentieth century might well take the *Leibnitz* of that time as his model. Outside was the sky and the wonderful salt air, while inside, on the middle deck, hundreds of people lay on rotting mattresses, packed so tight no one could put a spoon to his mouth without jostling his neighbor. There was no ventilation, not a single windowlike aperture, and the portholes were soldered shut. But the truly frightful place was the orlop, the lowest of the three decks. The air there was so thick it stifled the flames in the lanterns. The passengers waited in complete apathy. No one quarreled over meals anymore. People sucked on objects, and from time to time—perhaps—someone would descend from the limbo of the middle deck into this hell, to give food to one groaning mouth or another.

Wherever you looked there was human excrement. According to the New York Harbor Authority's report on the ship, there was not a handsbreadth of deck that was not soiled with vomit or fecal matter.

The poison breath of the orlop wafted more and more powerfully up to the middle deck, and since from time to time the screams of rats and of people could be heard, the upper passengers no longer dared to come down. When the dying began, the crew left the corpses to rot, removing them only when worms began to plague the survivors. Of course there was no priest on board (priests rarely emigrated), and so the dead were thrown overboard with a shout of "Heave-ho!" Hardly a day without deaths, on a voyage of nearly seventy days.

All this was confirmed by the Office of Commissioners of Immigration of the State of New York on January 22, 1868—eleven days after the ghost ship's arrival at dawn. One hundred eight out of 544 immigrants had died. The officials and doctors who were the first to climb on board were not received by the crew, nor by the captain, but by dozens of crying, exhausted children, who, when asked about their parents' whereabouts, answered by pointing over the railing: There! There!

At this point I would like to draw attention to the fact that only one member of the crew died—the cook; and that there was a girl who claimed, without tears or any sign of sorrow, that she was the daughter of the deceased cook.

The girl was presumed to be about thirteen or fourteen years old, though she claimed to be only twelve; and when asked for her name, she replied: "Maria."

Maria who?

The girl shook her head and answered: "Maria."

Maria was taken aside and placed like a relic next to

3

the customs officers. There she stood, motionless, watching the removal of the passengers, some of them dying even as they were carried away.

It was still snowing, and by the time the last man had stepped off the ship, the sky had laid a white shroud over the deck of the *Leibnitz*.

2

My name is Howard J. Ragcct. I am a fifty-cight-year-old pediatrician. I live on Riverside Drive, on the Upper West Side of Manhattan—a somewhat dilapidated but still dignified area (I'm speaking of architecture, comfort, and a certain degree of security); and until recently I ran my practice at home, too. When I leave the apartment to go to a concert or a movie, the uniformed doorman steps out onto the street with a whistle in his mouth and hails a cab for me, and I always return in a taxi. My wife died of leukemia two years ago. My two grown children live in Boston. The girl, Lea, unmarried as yet, is studying medicine; the boy, Randolph, is a pediatrician, like me.

I'm well aware of the snobbishness of doctors who think they belong to some kind of aristocracy just be-

5

cause their family has produced three generations of medical men. Well, so far my family has produced five generations who've taken the Hippocratic oath—an oath, incidentally, which at this time in my life I would pronounce only with eyes shut and fingers crossed. But let's not dwell on that.

A century ago my ancestors were living in Graubünden, Switzerland. (I know these matters well, having always had an interest in genealogy and things historical. I have even visited the place.) My great-grandfather emigrated from the Graubünden area shortly after the turn of the previous century. Before that, he had worked at the post office in his native village of Rhäzüns, taken his Latin exams from the village pastor, and gone on to study medicine in Stuttgart. He was still single when he left with a group of young compatriots, but after coming to America he married a Swiss woman.

It must have been a bitter time. A single snowy summer had brought hunger into the villages, which were already poor, and the young men had no choice but to serve in foreign armies, work in hotels or confectioneries in various European countries, or take the trip across the sea. In my great-grandfather's case, however, there must have been an ingredient of wanderlust and desire for adventure.

These notes are intended to provide an introduction to a ballad about the life and death of a beautiful creature named Mary Mallon, alias Typhoid Mary. Johann Wolfgang Goethe (who is not very well known in this country) granted a wide range of possibilities to the ballad form, which is why I've taken the liberty of calling my little biography a ballad. I am describing a life that began sadly—at a still tender age—then passed through low point after low point till it came to a silent and by no means lyrical end.

6

On November 11, 1938, the body of Mary Mallon was transported with almost hysterical haste to St. Raymond's Cemetery in the Bronx and buried there. No autopsy was performed. I found this out in an article by George A. Soper, Ph.D., "The Curious Career of Typhoid Mary" (*The Diplomate,* Dec. 1939). It's strange that Soper didn't publish his final report until one year after Mary's death. At any rate, it was George A. Soper who awakened my grandfather's interest in this woman's extraordinary fate. I have in my possession a calendar that my grandfather used as a sort of secret log to keep records on his own private research into Mary's case. He did this behind the back of his friend and colleague; in fact, I have reason to suspect that their friendship eventually foundered over this issue. Both were still young when this rivalry over a woman began, very young; and since Mary was considerably older, it's sensible to conclude that it was as a medical case that she fascinated them, not as a female. Soper's interest was strictly professional; for my grandfather it was more of a hobby. Soper, incidentally, published his first article about Mary as early as 1907.

I have made use of what little information I have been able to gather; all the rest of Mary's reality is my own invention. The fact that Mary Mallon, alias Maria Caduff, came from the region where my ancestors once lived was one of the reasons that prompted me to write this story. Another is the dubious advantage of having fallen prey to a treacherous disease that is giving me endless leisure time to kill.

3

Years before the great north European exodus began—mainly Irish and German immigrants—and before Ellis Island became an immigrants' processing center, most of the newly arrived were treated with as much contempt as they had experienced back home. Shabbily dressed, carrying pathetic little bundles, ignorant of their new homeland's language and (let's face it) unculture, they were received by sneering officials and cynical doctors, many of them quacks, who would have gladly accepted bribes if the immigrants, ragged and weakened in body and soul, had owned anything that might have tempted them. The few valuables they had brought along were mementos of the old country—rings, bracelets, tools of various trades—and what little money they had was intended to help them begin their new life.

8

Among the first sights to welcome the immigrants was the inside of a fortress, rebuilt to serve as an opera house, though it had served for dogfights as well. Hard-bitten wrestlers and boxers with bare fists had given performances there, along with fire eaters and screeching singers who had been chased off the stage in Vienna or Berlin. Castle Garden—the new name given Castle Clinton—had been an opera house for only a short time. It had reached its peak in the early 1850s, when the well-known Swedish coloratura soprano Jenny Lind honored the establishment with her presence. The end came soon after. The stage, designed to offer a platform for high culture, turned out to be much less interesting than the auditorium, with its six thousand seats and a standing-room capacity of four thousand, where members of the audience fleeced one another, shot craps, and slit open women's pocketbooks; where pimps paraded their underage merchandise, drunks beheaded their whiskey bottles on the backs of chairs, exhibitionists spread open their cloaks in the direction of the stage. Eventually the culture circus was shut down and its doors were sealed, and in 1855 the New York Immigration Authority decided to rebuild the place as a processing center for immigrants. Needless to say, there was little reconstruction. The trashy decor was stripped off, the chandeliers were auctioned, and with all the hammering, the stucco fell from the ceiling. The once luxurious lounges were turned into showers. No immigrant was permitted to set foot on the clean new land without taking a shower, and his clothes had to be disinfected in a steam oven before he was allowed to put them back on. Only then did the painful questions begin. Wherefrom? Whereto? Howcome? Howmuch?

* * *

Maria stood on the top deck of the *Leibnitz*, next to the two doctors and two immigration officers who had supervised the clearing of the ship. Her lips were blue from the cold, her fingers tightened into fists. One of the immigration officers issued an order to have the ship fumigated immediately. He then asked the other men which of them would volunteer to take the child through Castle Garden. He asked casually, hardly listening when someone suggested this was an awful thing to inflict on an orphaned girl. At just that moment the child ran across the deck. She slipped and fell on the ice-coated wood, got up immediately, and rushed toward the railing. The two doctors ran after and seized her. She flailed her arms and legs at them, bit and scratched them. A kick struck one of them in the face. Finally they overpowered her and pinned her to the deck.

The immigration officials stood and watched. They looked bored. "Listen, Doctor," said one of them in a tone of good-natured inhumanity, "maybe it would have been better for the kid . . ."

As chronicler of Maria's life, I have to admit it would have been better if she had died then. But fate came to her rescue, in the form of a doctor—of all possible disguises surely the most ironic, since this act of rescue, on the part of a man trained to save lives, would result in the death of hundreds, perhaps thousands more.

The two officials stepped onto the gangplank with equanimity; what they had seen was an everyday affair.

4

The older of the two doctors who had prevented Maria from jumping overboard was one Gerald Dorfheimer. Dorfheimer urged his colleague to follow the two customs officials who had just stepped off the ship; he, Dorfheimer, would take care of the girl. The other doctor was all too willing to escape—twilight, misery, death, and cold.

A few minutes later, a coast guard boat arrived, bringing a handful of men who climbed on board and grumpily went about their business. Dorfheimer asked the sailors who had stayed in the boat to row him and the girl ashore. They rowed back, paying no further attention to Dorfheimer or the girl.

The doctor took the child by the hand and led her through hallways and inspection booths, casually, as if she were his daughter. You could hear the muted din from inside Castle Garden. (There are, incidentally, officials at Ellis Island Museum who claim that at night you can still hear the screams of parents and children being separated; the *New York Post* just recently ran a story on it. Parapsychology?) Dorfheimer, who had no idea he was protecting a strangely predestined child, was without a doubt risking his license and his profession, though—as we shall see—his deed was not devoid of self-interest.

Occasionally I like to imagine a spaceship that fulfills the conditions of Einstein's theory, flying at the speed of light, bringing back the past, catching up with it, as it were; and I imagine the children I would take along with me to other galaxies. Oliver Twist would be one, and Holden Caulfield, Chaplin's "Kid," Huckleberry Finn and the Little Prince; also the child Arthur Rimbaud, the child Vincent van Gogh, the child Francisco Goya, the child Amadeo Modigliani, the child Abraham Lincoln, the child Hannibal, the child Wolfgang Amadeus Mozart, the child Rainer Maria Rilke, the children Janis Joplin and Oscar Wilde, all the unknown children of Auschwitz, maybe the child Adolf Hitler as well, who perhaps wouldn't have got into fights with the child Mao Tse-tung. I would have deprived the world of much of its so-called good and much of its so-called evil as well, but my spaceship—call it childish, if you like— would have left the world poorer.

And the child Maria, would I have taken her too? Yes, without a doubt . . .

At the time of her arrival (to come back to Earth) we may imagine her as a rather sturdy peasant girl, emaci-

12

ated by misery and deprivation, dressed in an ill-fitting short skirt, with a cap pulled down to her eyebrows.

Maria had adopted a comical sort of sailor's lurch during the trip overseas. But her cool eyes and her fingers cramped like claws suggested the silent watchfulness of a cat.

5

It was noon when Dorfheimer found a coach in a side street near the Battery, after leading Mary by the hand through a noisy crowd of vendors, sailors, shopkeepers, and ragged children. The filth on the ground was ankle-deep and laced with slush from the night's snowfall, pale brown and grainy like barley meal. Deals were being closed in the harbor, mostly crooked deals, needless to say. Fathers, just released with their kin from the grotesque opera house and beginning their search for shelter, were lured into bars by friendly innkeepers, pumped full of alcohol, and robbed; others bought land that no one except for some faraway Indians had ever laid eyes on.

Swindling and sharp practice, briefly contained dur-ing the years of the Civil War, were now spreading

14

again with pestilential rapidity. The sea wind blew
stinking clouds of sulfur into lower Manhattan from
recently docked ships that had to be disinfected. The
war that had ravaged the South had turned the port of
New York into a mountain of merchandise, and behind
it there towered a forest of masts, which in but a few
years would be replaced by the chimneys of steamships.

Maria sat with a stony face next to Dorfheimer. Later
on, people in the streets would reappear in her dreams:
goat, sheep, and dog faces; frog and snake faces; pig
faces. How unimaginative our eyes become once we
have outgrown our childhood . . .

New York is the oldest city in the world.

On the East Side (near today's Twenty-sixth Street)
Dorfheimer pressed a few coins into the coachman's
palm and told him Maria had fallen asleep. He tried to
wake her up by whispering into her ear and stroking her
lids with his fingers. The coachman watched him impa-
tiently over his shoulder, clicked his tongue, and sup-
pressed a curse. Dorfheimer carefully cradled the back

of Maria's neck in the crook of his right arm. He was not a particularly strong man, and he looked up with an almost relieved expression when his housekeeper, a sixty-year-old matron, appeared at the door of the house with her hands on her hips, streaks of flour and batter on her bare arms. She made no motion to help the doctor.

"Vicky!"

Vicky obeyed, not without hesitation, though finally she took the child from his arms like a doll, glanced at her face—with repugnance, it seemed—and carried her inside.

"Please put her to bed right away," Dorfheimer said. He blinked in embarrassment when Vicky asked how old the girl was. He didn't know exactly, he said, maybe thirteen or a little bit older.

He breathed heavily, stopped for a moment under the door, and then stepped into a small vestibule, where he hung his hat and coat under a gold-framed picture of the President. He stopped again at the door to the dining room and turned uncertainly—almost as if he were asking his housekeeper's permission to step into the room.

"Your lunch is ready, Doctor," Vicky called down from the upper staircase.

"And the child?" he asked with a subdued voice.

Vicky did not answer. She was making an audible effort to drag the girl into the bathroom, and Maria's voice, groaning in a kind of sleepy stupor, irritated him.

"Vicky," he called, but she didn't seem to hear him. He sat down at the table, hesitant and lost in thought, scraped a dab of butter with the tip of his knife on a charred piece of toast, and pushed aside the food, which had grown cold.

He rose to his feet and climbed up the stairs with a

heavy tread, past small gold-framed engravings showing German cities, stopping to look at each picture with an expression of surprise and politeness. He was tired.

He opened the drawer of his night table and pulled out a book that had recently become famous in England and subsequently in America. Dorfheimer was particularly fascinated that the book had been written by a teacher of mathematics: *Alice's Adventures in Wonderland*.

6

That is how Maria arrived in the New World. There was a moment when she heaved out of sleep, screaming because she no longer heard the thundering of the sea, the groaning and creaking of masts and planks; she looked around with astonishment and fell asleep again. Vicky spent hours by her bedside, occasionally held a glass of peppermint tea to her lips and stuffed little pieces of biscuit into her half-opened mouth, which chewed mechanically while Mary continued to sleep.

Dorfheimer got up toward evening and dressed in a hurry, and was about to leave for night duty when Vicky came downstairs and helped him into his coat.

"There's something you want to tell me, Vicky, isn't there? What is it?"

"How did the child get off the boat, and who does she belong to?"

"We'll talk about it another time, Vicky," he answered, and went to the door.

A dry, icy wind was blowing as Dorfheimer walked down Fifth Avenue. Usually he took a route farther east, down Fourth or Third Avenue. The avenues with their four- and five-story houses were not yet cluttered with wildly crisscrossing telephone and telegraph wires.

What actually did the world look like at that time, and what was going on?

Ludwig I, the king of Bavaria, had passed away. In Cuba, there was a rebellion against the Spanish. Here in America, Negroes had been granted the right to vote. Richard Wagner finished *Die Meistersinger von Nürnberg* and Brahms his choral work *A German Requiem;* and in the wretchedly blissful, blissfully wretched world of religion, the stern Lutherans closed ranks at the General Lutheran Conference, while the Vatican prepared for its twentieth ecumenical council.

Midnight is approaching as I write these lines. As my sickness progresses I note, not without gratitude, the degree to which writing is proving its usefulness as an anesthetic. But that's neither here nor there. I don't plan to record the details of my own case history.

Outside I can hear the various ill-boding sirens howling their human concern with such insistence. Police cars, fire trucks, ambulances—the only true processionals in America, according to Oscar Wilde, who turned up here a few years after Mary's arrival.

Night sounds were different back then. Fire wagons

19

clanged a bell as they drove by, and instead of a police siren you'd hear the shrill screech of a copper's whistle. The person running past you gasping for breath would not be a jogger, but probably a lawbreaker testing his fitness against the pursuing police.

Lawbreakers—Dorfheimer gave a start: no, he was not a lawbreaker! Anyone forced to witness the inhuman bureaucracy at Castle Garden for years on end, night after night and day after day, could surely be excused if just occasionally he applied a saw to the iron bars of that system. Dorfheimer had saved two married couples, one from Germany and one from Poland, by tampering with their medical reports; saved their children as well, who by law were supposed to be separated from their parents if found ill. Twice he had saved little girls from a stay in an orphanage during their parents' quarantine, by giving them lodging in his home. He could have lost his license from some of these good deeds; but to call them licentious would have been going too far.

At any rate, he had always taken care to cloak his special sort of kindness toward little girls in the guise of a more general human kindness. Apparently Vicky did not see it that way. An undesirable thought, which he quickly got rid of.

7

When Dorfheimer came
home from work shortly before midnight, the sight of
two leather suitcases standing in the doorway gave him
a fright. A note lay on top of one of the suitcases: "Will
be picked up.—V. L."

Every room of the house was lit, and attached to the
hook where he usually hung his coat and hat was a
letter. It was from Vicky—he immediately recognized
her stiffly vertical, unsteady handwriting. "Dear Dr.
Dorfheimer, you know I'm not nosy, even though you
are a bachelor, still not married. However, I can't go on
watching you and your tendencies any longer, coming
as I do from a decent family. My brother-in-law will
pick up my bags in a few days. Enclosed is the shopping money, 22 Dollars. I expect no further pay. Re-

spectfully yours Vicky L." There was a P.S.: "The child was still fast asleep, I didn't want to wake her. Best wishes to you despite everything."

Dorfheimer's hands trembled. He read the letter four or five times and tore it up. A teapot stood on the dressing table, two hard-boiled eggs with their shells removed, and a pastrami sandwich, mustard, pepper, and salt. He took a bite without sitting down, chewed listlessly. Finally he went up the stairs, treading extra softly on the dark red runner to keep the boards from creaking. He stopped in front of Maria's room, pressed his ear to the door, listened. He heard her breathing evenly.

The door to Vicky's room had been left half open; still, he listened before opening the door all the way. The room was so neat it looked as though no one had ever lived in it. Vicky had taken her parakeet, Cindy, and it was this more than anything that gave him a ridiculous feeling of abandonment. A silly bird who kept screeching "How are you today?" and always answered itself with "Thank you, sir, I'm fine."

Outside, the wind was driving the snow in an almost horizontal direction. Dorfheimer's room was positively Spartan. It was the only room in the house where no pictures were hung. As usual, Vicky had drawn the suffocatingly heavy velvet curtains and uncovered a geometrically perfect triangle of white linen. On the console stood a menorah without candles and a daguerreotype portrait of his mother: penumbral. An arm's length from his bed stood a second bed, which he had bought when he set up house eleven years ago. He had been briefly engaged.

On the night table to his left burned a kerosene lamp set on low flame. Vicky had put a glass of water next to the lamp, and next to the glass—as usual—a bottle of bourbon, as well as a second, smaller glass. He took off his clothes, pulled a dressing gown around his shoulders, and sat down on the edge of the bed. Then he hastily poured himself a glass of whiskey, emptied it, filled it again, emptied and filled it a third and fourth time, without pleasure, pulling down the corners of his mouth, exactly as if it were medicine. He examined his naked feet. They were very clean, white, with a reddish flush and pale blue veins. They looked smug to him. Not distinguished, there's no such thing as a distinguished foot, but just smug, coddled. He filled the water glass with bourbon, up to the edge, and poured it down.

He did not notice that an hour had gone by, and then a second hour. He had let himself sink down sideways, leaning an elbow against the pillow and trying to visualize Maria's face and figure.

Finely limbed, yet strong; the long Botticelli neck. Delicate hands coarsened by hard work, ruddy, chapped, and scarred. Light gray eyes, which took on a glowering expression beneath brows contracted with effort. Her gait, the movements of her arms, still awkward, rough-hewn. Light blond hair falling into her brow. He remembered her hips, already beginning to fill out beneath the waist, and this thought frightened him as severely as if he had stumbled over his own shadow.

8

When he came downstairs in the morning, Maria was standing behind one of the high chairs in the dining room, immobile, her hands arranged on the back of the chair, as if a photographer had posed her that way. She had put on a dressing gown which he, Dorfheimer, had once worn. Her hair was carefully combed.

"Hello, Maria" was the good-natured, casual greeting he wanted to give her, but the words stuck in his throat, and all that came out was a hoarse "Hello."

"Hello," replied Maria. He stood still, uncertain of how to proceed, while she went out into the kitchen, awkward in her long gown, and returned with a dish of scrambled eggs and toast she had been keeping warm on the stove.

24

"I suppose Vicky gave you instructions, eh?" He asked the question in German, then shook his head at himself, for, apart from her brief struggle with Vicky in the bathtub, Mary could scarcely have taken any notice of his housekeeper.

Instead of replying, Maria resumed her position, hands decoratively posed on the back of the chair. Her pale eyes gazed steadily at a point above and beyond his head.

"Vicky was the housekeeper," he said, almost apologetically, and began buttering his toast. "Wouldn't you like to sit down, and especially, wouldn't you like to eat?"

She shook her head and remained standing.

"You're from southern Germany or Switzerland, am I correct?" She fixed an unblinking gaze on him, as if she failed to understand a single word. "From Switzerland," he repeated. "From Graubünden, though you lived in Germany part of the time with two sisters. I mean you helped out on a farm in Schwaben during the summers— you were what they call a *Schwabengängerin*."

Maria stared at a spot on the wall behind him.

"I looked it up in the ship's registry," he continued, listlessly poking at his scrambled eggs. "You understand some English, I know that, but Sean Mallon, the cook, was not your father."

She said nothing.

"I assume your parents and your sisters died of the epidemic during the crossing. Cholera or typhoid fever."

Mary gave no answer.

"You can live with . . . you can live in this house. I'll find a school for you, a nice school. Can you read and write?"

She twisted her mouth, sucked in her lower lip, did not answer. Dorfheimer decided he could interpret this as "Yes."

"Soon I'll find someone to replace Vicky. Someone motherly, someone you'll like, hm? Tell me, Maria— how old are you?"

This time something like a smile moved her lips. She was intelligent, you could tell: she had shown this shadow of a smile because she realized that Dorfheimer could have easily found the answer to his question in the ship's register. She did not move.

"The orphanages in this city are terrible. Here in this house you'll have everything you need. Upstairs in Vicky's room there's a Sears & Roebuck catalog, you can make an *x* next to whatever you'd like to have and we'll have it shipped over here. Or, if you prefer, we could go shopping together tomorrow, hm?"

She did not move.

Did she smile? No. She didn't smile, she grinned. Dorfheimer was taken aback, because in his view of the world young girls of that age did not grin.

"Well, do you want to?" He tried to suppress his disappointment, his hidden anger, and this time he joined in her silence, pushing a piece of toast into his mouth.

Then, unexpectedly, she came out with a sentence, a single one, and in English. She said: "I can cook."

He took a deep breath.

"Good," he said, continuing in German. "I have to hurry now. There's some money over there, a few dollars Vicky left. Buy yourself whatever you need. To wear, or to cook." He laughed. "There's a key lying next to the money, it fits the front door. And watch out that you don't get lost. This is an evil city we live in."

He walked up to her and kissed her on the forehead. The forehead seemed as cool as her eyes, which looked up at him quickly. He went to the hallway, put on his coat, and left the house.

"Plague on board! Plague on board! Ships bring plague from Europe!" The newsboys shouted their lungs sore beneath their skinny dog-ribs.

9

A few words about the times:
there are many cities whose wealth shines with a stellar
glare comparable to that of New York, but in no other
Western city does the sight of poverty assault you with
such insulting, provocative insistence. Here a rich man
needs all the callousness that was tanned and talcumed
into his soul-hide by the combined influences of the
nursery and the Christian faith. Little by little, a frame
of mind develops that leaves no room for even so much
as indifference, just enough for a bland affirmation of
the unalterable. Wealth is anesthetized toothache. A
painless pain.

And I—in my comfortable armchair at my desk—am
actually leafing through books to find out what poverty
looked like a hundred years ago. A lot more romantic,

27

from our point of view; a lot more bizarre and exotic.

I just opened a book to a contemporary drawing of a ragpicker. Now why would a ragpicker pick rags? Surely not in order to deliver them to the textile industry for recycling. No, he hocked his rags to people who were even poorer than he. For ten cents you could spend the night in a flophouse, a barracks with nowhere near enough room to provide lodging for the crowds that piled in every evening; the sleeping bodies lay stacked side by side, literally like sardines. Snow and cold came blowing in through the cracks, and only those who managed to lie near the tiny metal stove need not have feared freezing. The owner of the flophouse didn't make a terrific living, but a living it was, a living off other people's misery. A foggy steam rose from the manholes in the streets—the refuse of wealth, expelled from the pipes of steam-heated buildings. Homeless children squatted around these steaming circles during winter nights; in the old pictures you can see well-fed

gentlemen walking past these huddling derelicts, gentlemen in furs, puffing on cigars.

Strange: in America both the poor *and* the rich believe in an immanent, divinely appointed justice.

Little Italian boys who had been bought or simply abducted from their native country were taught how to sing and play the violin to the crack of a whip—and this by people to whom the name Stradivarius meant a brand of wine, if they recognized it at all.

Poverty in southern climes is said to disturb the observer's cultivated eye less than it does in the north with its icy winters. But here in New York the summer is horrible as well. While in the mass shelters lice and bedbugs were already snuggling in for the good season to come, the poorest of the poor languished on the pavement, gasping, usually with little success, for the slightest stirring of air from the sea. Was the sea holding its breath for sheer horror? And every morning began with the shouting, ranting, and cursing of business. Heavy-laden carts rattled through the streets, and woe to anyone not yet alert nor instantly master of his limbs—for soon he'd become their slave.

It was through such quarters that Dorfheimer walked to work, well-to-do, self-assured, full of pity. Still, all he could think of was Maria. Maria—kidnapped, yes, but for the best of motives. A humane, a benevolent crime. Dorfheimer was not an atheist. He merely doubted his own faith in God.

Just a moment ago my daughter, Lea, called me on the phone: "What's up, Doc?"

"I'm fine," I said. Then there was a pause, and I thought the call had been interrupted, but it was just awkwardness on her part. Then she went on to ask how my manuscript was coming.

"Fine," I said again, and she laughed. When you ask a physician after the state of his health, it's a little like stepping into the hangman's house and requesting a rope.

10

When Dorfheimer returned
—in the evening this time—the house was filled with a
delicious smell. Delicious because even a meal prepared out of barley, bacon, and string beans can smell
delicious, and Dorfheimer cried out, no, he roared with
enthusiasm: "Ha!"

There was no one in the kitchen. He went to the
dining room, where the table was set, as if against all
expectation Vicky had decided to come home. Three
candles were lit on the table. But no sight of Maria.

"Maria."

No answer. He stood still for a moment, hesitating,
then mechanically hung his coat on the hook and called,
this time with a softer, more questioning voice: "Maria?"

Had Vicky in fact returned? Penitent? An affected

31

throat-clearing sound could be heard from the top floor.

"Maria?"

Dorfheimer slowly walked up the stairs. There was light shining out from the half-opened door of his bedroom. He stopped. Maria was sitting on the edge of his bed. She was wearing a rather vulgar and outsized lady's dress, and she was holding her feet inside a steaming copper basin. There was a smell of sheep's or goat's fat. She was watching him. No smile. Just that frightening grin again. He went to the bathroom like a nurse reprimanded by her superior, fetched some towels, dried her calves first, then her feet, muttering reproachfully to himself: how could he, a doctor, not have realized how delicate the state of her health might be, what with that frightful sea voyage and the cold and those many weeks of deprivation. He was babbling.

Maria stroked his hair, and when he looked up she was grinning again, and he kissed her knee and the tender skin above the knee, the inside of her thighs, and gradually groped his way toward the curves of her upper body, quivering with desire; and finally she pulled his chin up to her with her hand, and made a sniffing face, the way you would demonstrate the idea of sniffing to a deaf-mute child. He looked up at her, dumbfounded, as if he did not comprehend that the nose is not an independent sense organ, and stared at her grinning mouth. "I can cook," she said, and Dorfheimer stood up, as if profoundly insulted.

He walked swiftly downstairs, took the pot off the stove, burning his fingers, and carried the meal into the dining room, where he discovered that Maria had set the table for herself as well as for him. That surprised him, because he had imagined himself dining as his own solitary guest, just as he always did.

Should he sit down?

"Maria!" he called. "Everything's ready."

Silence.

"Maria!" He put the three middle fingers of his right hand around his left wrist and forced himself to count a hundred pulsebeats. Then he went back upstairs. His face had turned pale, and he stood still, breathing deeply.

Maria was naked. The awful dress lay on the floor, whorishly purple, and the white pillow was placed as if accidentally in such a way as to cover her loins.

As soon as he leaned down to kiss her, she put on her grin again. He awkwardly took off his clothes, lay down next to her, and stroked her childish face. To his astonishment, she began to stroke him. Was she really still a child? Not until he finally tried to penetrate her did that grin turn into a smile.

Once again, the end came abruptly. His manhood collapsed, and Maria's grin returned, a grin which she seemed to be flaunting and which seemed to contain the derision of all the women of this world. He didn't suffer. On the contrary. He turned over onto his back. Where and from whom had she learned this, he asked. Was it that Irish ship's cook?

She nodded. Silence. She was just a little over thirteen years old, an age at which other children still played with dolls, and she had neither parents nor a home, and in her face you could see the childhood she had lost, as you can in photographs of children taken during wartime. All of a sudden Dorfheimer felt ashamed of his nakedness and reached for his clothes. Maria pulled the sheet up to her chin and stared at the ceiling.

After a while he could tell by her breathing that once again she had fallen into her deep, childish sleep.

Dorfheimer couldn't sleep that night.

11

Apart from her room and the stairway leading up to it, Maria was frightened by the general darkness of the house, which was perhaps due to the ruling taste of the time. Everything here looked high-class to Maria, all the bric-a-brac of pseudo-Greek, Elizabethan-Victorian pomp with Japanese netsuke, Meissen porcelain, Anglo-Chinese colonial frippery, Christian humble-pie rococo, French plush chaise longues, Rogers groups for the round table in the guest room, gold-framed monstrosities with the inextinguishable glaze of established cretinism in their beady eyes. And everywhere family albums with gilded edges and vases full of wax flowers.

The days came and went. Maria inhabited the kitchen, with plates lining its walls just as books lined the walls of the doctor's study. There were utensils in this kitchen whose meaning she could not at first divine: spoons that were too large for the usual purpose spoons were put to, and various technical contraptions for the upper-middle-class kitchen of those days. But it didn't take long for her to discover how and when to employ them. She studied cookbooks that had once belonged to Dorfheimer's mother, read them for hours, without tiring. Maria had no dictionary, but with the help of the illustrations and her own native imagination, she soon recognized the European equivalents and succeeded in understanding several recipes, committing them to memory before she had even tested them.

The kitchen may have been her kingdom, but it was a private one. It did not take long for her to find her way around her immediate neighborhood, and to get to know the people there, and their names as well, and soon she too was known to the others as Maria, even though she rarely answered their questions with more than a nod or a shake of the head. She let the English language grow inside her, and only when she was sure she was alone in the house did she call out the words she had recently acquired and try to articulate them with the playful perseverance by which children learn. She loved life in the streets and the people—those raucous, ruthless, puking, cursing, spitting, magnificent, shameless, mean, brutalized, underhanded, simple-minded, shrewd, deceived, disloyal people who traded and plied their crafts there.

"Caaaarpets . . . Caaaarpets . . . Caaaarpets . . ."

"Glaaasss . . . Glaaasss . . . Glaaasss . . ."

"Straight from the udder . . . Fresh cow's milk . . ."

And the grunting of pigs led to market. And the roared and shouted praises of anything picked, plucked, harvested, shot, or slaughtered to fill a stomach, and curses in countless languages flung back and forth between competing vendors, with garbled bits of English thrown in. Maria inspected the meat with the critical, knowing gaze of an old hand in the kitchen, scrutinizing the flies that crawled over a calf's liver until the butcher shouted at her, insulted. The women behind their vegetable stalls gave her cooking tips. She took it all in as if she were learning poems in a foreign language, and listened openmouthed to the women in the fish market laughing, swearing, scraping the scales off the fish and shrieking obscenities, almost none of which Maria could understand. Anything even remotely related to cooking attracted her special attention, and whenever she came across some odor she could not identify, she would linger until someone grew curious and asked her a question. Dorfheimer ate very little of the dishes Maria attempted to cook for him. He always praised her.

One morning Dorfheimer failed to get up. He had a fever, his eyes were tearing, he was rolling from side to side. Maria administered rose-hip tea, and the liquid flowed in rivulets down his chin and neck. His eyes began to stare and look expressionless even as they followed her movements with quick jerks and stops. The smell of feces spread through the room. Maria filled a basin with hot water, exactly as if she had learned it in a hospital. She tried to pull the sweat-soaked sheets out from under him. He was too heavy for her, despite his delicate build. She kept the windows shut. Outside, a pile of snow was building up against the glass in the lower window frame.

At dinnertime she carried a plate full of soup with a spoon up the stairs and put it on the little table by his bedside. The way a cat will bring a dead mouse to its master's or mistress's bed, as a sign of affection.

The following morning Maria heard the ding-dong of the bell on the front door and saw a man's silhouette through its porcelain-glass panes. She did not open the

door. The visitor returned an hour later, knocked against the window with a cane or an umbrella. She didn't move.

At five in the afternoon, Dorfheimer lay in agony, whispering nursery rhymes, and when she came back to his room at half past six, he was dead.

Maria had observed, on the *Leibnitz*, how a rag is wrapped around a dead person's head and jaw so the chin doesn't stay hanging open, and she had also observed how the eyes of the dead are pressed shut. She folded his hands in an attitude of prayer, stood by the feet of the deceased, mumbling a prayer, amen, carried the plate with the cold soup back down to the kitchen, and returned with a few wax flowers to place on his bed. Then she wrapped two silver candlesticks in a tablecloth, together with a rococo porcelain statuette of a girl whose reddish hair had delighted her. Several dollar bills and some coins lay in the kitchen. She pocketed the money, wrapped a scarf around her neck, and pulled the woolen hat all the way down to her eyes. Then she took a sheet of paper, went over the words in her mind a few times, and wrote: "Mr. Dorfheimer is dad. Bleeze halp him."

She carefully shut the front door, turned the key twice, and then threw it into the snow.

She disappeared in the crowd, walking with small, seemingly purposeful steps.

Where to?

12

The snow fell and fell, as if to keep a meteorological contract, and the people stumped along, Indian file, in their predecessors' footsteps.

Maria stopped in front of a low wooden house on Twenty-third Street, the vegetable store of Mrs. Alma Newton, whom she had gotten to know in the course of her shopping expeditions. Alma Newton was a thin, elderly compatriot from eastern Switzerland. She, too, had worked for German farmers as a *Schwabengängerin* when she was a child, and it was with this woman, and only with her, that Maria occasionally chatted in the dialect of her native Graübunden.

Alma Newton could use her, she knew that. For Alma had been struck by a very special misfortune. Her husband, Gilbert Newton, had been the successful proprietor of an apple orchard in New Jersey for more than twenty years—until two years ago, in 1866, when he discovered that his workers had forgotten to harvest one of his richly blessed apple trees. A peculiar accident, or else a deliberate oversight; at any rate, Mr. Newton paid a miserable price for it. He fetched a ladder, and no sooner had he placed it against the trunk of the tree than the apples came rattling down pell-mell, a hailstorm, an avalanche of autumn fruit, which knocked him into a state of unconsciousness from which he would never awaken. Conceivably some fists had been added for good measure.

The doctors believed that Mr. Newton might go on living for years without ever getting well again. His eyes were wide open, but no one could tell whether he could hear, see, or understand anything of what was happening around him. He lay there like a reptile, letting his tongue dart out once in a while. Every few hours he had to be spoon-fed a few gulps of soup, which he swallowed with much messy slavering and with apparent reluctance.

Since Alma Newton had spent a good part of her childhood doing hard work for very little reward, and since she considered a life without work a life lived in disgrace, she quite rightly did not regard this spoon-feeding chore as genuine work, and though she loved her husband, she would rather have seen him dead. Yes, would Maria take care of him? She could earn four dollars a week in addition to food and board. She'd be expected to clean up in the house a bit, too, of course, and, well, yes, the sick man.

Maria accepted the offer without hesitation, and while she helped Alma peel apples she could hear Mr. Newton's throat rattling upstairs. It was something you

41

could get used to quickly, and Alma's applesauce, which they were busy preparing, was considered a delicacy in that part of town.

With a sigh Alma said it was time to feed the sick man. Maria immediately got up and hurried to the kitchen. All she had to do was warm it up, Alma called after her. "It" was a gray potato broth, into which Alma would usually stir an egg just before bringing the soup to a boil. Maria, however, poured the contents of the saucepan down the drain. Was there any barley, she shouted back—any beans, any bacon?

What? Nonsense! "None of this fancy cooking," came Alma's reply. She had no idea how shocked and almost offended Maria was at finding in Alma's kitchen not one of the simple ingredients that would have gone into a Sunday meal in the country they both came from. Soon the girl calmed down and prepared a soup—out of leeks, a little flour, and some lard—saltless, unfortunately, on doctor's orders. Maria wondered whatever doctors could possibly understand about salt. "Bad for his health!" Alma shouted, as if she had guessed her thoughts. How could anything still be good for his health, Maria wondered, and decided to obey her inner calling as a cook. No good soup without salt.

The feeding itself was not very appetizing. Maria adjusted the pillow behind Mr. Newton's back, pulled him up a bit by his shoulders. Mr. Newton's immobile gaze was fixed on Maria's left ear. He slurped, pulled back his tongue, snapped his mouth shut, opened it again, like an old sick bird, waiting for his next spoonful. After eleven or twelve helpings he clicked his teeth together as a sign that he had had enough.

"Tomorrow you'll get some real bean-and-barley soup," Maria whispered. "I mean real soup." And then, defiantly and even more softly: "I can cook!"

Mr. Newton did not answer, of course, but he did continue to observe her left ear, and finally, inadvertently, she raised her hand to touch her earlobe with her fingers. Yes, it was still there.

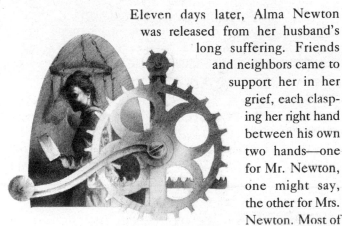

Eleven days later, Alma Newton was released from her husband's long suffering. Friends and neighbors came to support her in her grief, each clasping her right hand between his own two hands—one for Mr. Newton, one might say, the other for Mrs. Newton. Most of these people were poor, and since it was winter and flowers were expensive, many of the mourning guests brought a book from the old country or else dried meat or cake.

Everyone had heard of Maria's help and asked where she was. Alma raised her shoulders in bewilderment, told them how she had found her house in immaculate condition, the kitchen cleaner than it had ever been, how Maria had even folded the hands of the deceased and drawn the sheet over his head. She had tidied her own room, too. And she'd put a piece of paper on the floor and placed the house key on top as a weight, and on the paper, in a childish scrawl, it said: "Sorry! Mary, the cook."

Perhaps, some people suggested, she had found her

lost parents or relatives. Alma nodded and then turned her attention to the two men who were carrying the coffin to the top floor. She wondered whether these were helpers hired by the funeral home, and, if so, whether she might give them each a preserve-glass full of applesauce by way of a tip.

If Maria did not show up or send word by next spring, Alma said, she would write to some people they both knew back home. But actually she didn't for one moment think of doing such a thing, and the very next day she began a new life with the apple picker who had found Gilbert Newton unconscious under the tree.

To this day, the code of criminal law does not include a Newtonian law of gravitation pertaining to apple trees, and neither was the fortune of earth's children given its bitter taste by an apple.

Although in the course of my story I intend to give due allowance to the few biographical data George A. Soper was able to establish, and though I have my grandfather's calendar notes to consult, there's a good deal of uninhabited space left over, an emptiness that requires filling out. In short, a certain amount of the truth will have to be invented, for—as everyone knows—there is no such thing in this world as a true or authentic biography. There exists an unalterable substance, like sand in an hourglass. The various biographies always turn one and the same clock upside down, and the same sand will pour in an ever new sequence from one vessel into the other.

Mary Mallon, as she will be called from now on, was born under the name of Maria Anna Caduff. I myself came across this name (along with the names of her parents and siblings, of course) in the parish church and chancery of the congregation of Graubünden, and since the date of her emigration very nearly coincides with the date of her embarcation, there can be no doubt as to her identity; quite apart from the fact that a family of five with the surname Caduff was registered in the passenger list of the *Leibnitz*.

Mary Mallon was, as we all are, at first without fault and without blame. She was an angel of death. And this angel Mary was forced to lead a pitiful, indeed miserably mean and wretched existence, and brought great misfortune to many people, in culpable innocence.

Dr. George A. Soper never concerned himself with this moral question, and neither did my grandfather. As I've already said, both these men were interested only in the medical phenomenon that became popularly known as "Typhoid Mary"—without a doubt the most famous typhoid carrier of all time. Due to her truly unfortunate vocation—a passion for cooking, which no one and nothing could stifle—her impact was so devastating that most of her contemporaries assumed she must be an invention, not unlike Kilroy, the military monster who made his appearance not long after her death.

Typhoid Mary is not an invention. Her victims were put in real coffins and buried, and were often mourned with genuine tears. It is hard to determine their precise number, as George A. Soper himself points out, for who can trace all the ramifications of an epidemic?

Typhoid (Greek: fog) fever was and is a specifically human infectious disease that today, thanks to antibiotics, is fatal in only 2 to 3 percent of all cases; but a hundred or more years ago the mortality rate was much higher. The infection is precipitated by *Salmonella typhosa*, a bacterium first described by Eberth and Gaffky in 1880, that is usually transmitted by impure food or water and generally affects young people more readily than the old.

The symptoms of typhoid fever appear one to three weeks after infection: headaches and pain in the extremities, a general dimming or occlusion of consciousness, nosebleeds, chills, and a fever that rises each day by steady accretion until it hovers at an almost unvarying 104 degrees, while the feeling of sickness increases constantly. The patient becomes bloated and constipated, the salivary glands dry up, the spleen can be clearly felt. The lymph follicles of the intestines grow ulcerous and begin to disintegrate, and this may be followed later on by diarrhea the color and consistency of watery pea soup, and finally by intestinal bleeding or a rupturing of the intestinal wall accompanied by peritonitis.

The infected individual's feces contain millions of viable typhoid bacteria. These, after being transferred to food and beverages, frequently by flies and other insects, are the usual source of infection.

Should we attach symbolic significance to the fact that a fly never contracts typhus? Mary too never contracted the disease; it never became virulent in her body. She was a carrier and therefore a transmitter of typhoid, but medical science at that time had no knowledge of typhoid carriers—though a certain Robert Koch in Germany was beginning to have an inkling of it. Had he heard of Mary Mallon, she would almost certainly have been to him an angel of death only in the lyrical sense of the term. And to me?

Death is every doctor's hated neighbor. As a young practitioner you ignore him at first, later you nod politely when your paths cross, and finally you greet each other with cool professional courtesy. In my work as a

47

pediatrician I used to watch this inescapable neighbor, examine him with unconcealed detestation from his bony heel to the tip of his scythe, asking myself why I had not become a gerontologist. But to this day—and I am not very old yet, only fifty-eight, as I've already mentioned—I have not regretted it.

My sickness, too, will have no dealings with old age. In a few months or weeks that neighbor of mine will stop suddenly instead of passing me by as usual, and tip his hat in a highly un-American manner. The reader will, I hope, forgive me after this digression if I permit myself a less than reverent manner of describing death and the process of dying. As things stand, my reverence is still reserved for life itself.

14

If you look at pictures of New York from the seventies and eighties of the previous century, you get a ghostly impression of emptiness and void, which a moment later reveals itself as, simply, an absence of people. This is especially the case in photographs of elegant or otherwise special locations, for photographers of the time felt the sight of crowds outside their mansions might offend the inner life of their clients. One good example is a picture lying in front of me now, a photograph of the corner of City Hall and Chambers Street, which was no doubt taken at a very early Sunday morning hour, when not even the poor were on their way to church yet.

I imagine Mary appearing there. I picture the way

49

she admires the lively ladies and gentlemen in their horse-drawn carriages.

It was early in the evening, and she had nowhere to go. She had packed her bundle into a pretty straw basket, and halted irresolutely when an elderly man in livery, unquestionably a "gentleman" in Mary's eyes, came up and accosted her. And she allowed it, for she and the gentleman happened to be standing beneath a gas lantern, which clearly meant that the man addressing her was not to be counted among the riffraff that shunned the light.

"Where to, young lady?" A rhetorical question for starters, and then a direct one: "Are you perhaps seeking the company of two elderly gentlemen who would like to admire you and, um"—here he hesitated for a moment—"eventually entertain you royally, and reward you, hm?"

Mary did not reply. It was better to keep silent if one did not have ready a definite answer. The liveried gentleman seemed to have been waiting here for a long time, for you could see he was freezing. His nose was running, and his shoes were soiled with muddy slush.

"I'm a cook," Mary finally said, but the man in livery brushed the words away with his hand, burrowed in his breast pocket, and produced—as if by way of identification—a dollar bill, uncreased, seemingly fresh off the press. In her excitement Mary was no more able to judge its worth than his.

"A certain discretion is of course required," he added. When Mary asked whether she might be permitted to spend the night in this house, he smiled. "Come, come," he said in a fatherly manner—if she really was seeking a position as a cook, that could certainly be discussed the next day, or even that very evening.

"How old are you anyway, child?" he asked—not, we may be sure, to avoid recruiting what today's laws would define as a "minor."

Frightened, Mary told him her age by holding up all the fingers of two hands and then, somewhat indefinitely, a few of the fingers of one hand.

"What a lovely age," he said. He put his arm around her, very tactfully, and repeated his offer. "The two gentlemen are passionately fond of playing chess on Friday evenings, and I'm sure they would be overjoyed by such a dainty diversion." His hand exerted a slight pressure, and finally she followed him without argument.

The house was not exactly a gentleman's house— though Mary, of course, did not notice this. The foyer had seen its best days long ago. Shabby and worn leather easy chairs stood around as if salvaged from a theater basement; and glaring down from the walls was a rogue's gallery of red-cheeked, slit-eared lawyers, politicians, or "ancestors" who no doubt had been squatting in heaven for the past several decades as if it were some third-class rail depot. The fireplace was lit, and its warm wavering light illuminated the faces of the two gentlemen, who happened to be discussing their absolutely charming grandchildren over a bottle of bourbon. They looked very much like models posing for the sort of newspaper ad that was fashionable at the time. They turned around abruptly when their servant announced, with a bow and a voice subdued but still audible enough for aged ears: "Gentlemen—a young lady!"

"How delightful," cried one, and the other echoed him with a question: "Delightful, eh?"

"Thanks, Ferguson," said the gentleman, and Mary's discoverer withdrew, quietly closing the door behind him.

One of the men relieved her of her straw basket and carried it to the couch, waddling along in his slippers and chuckling over this visit, so late they had almost stopped hoping: "Yes, almost gave up on you, heh, heh, but you're certainly welcome. So tell us, child, where are you from?" He caressed her chin. "I'm Uncle Delbert, and the gentleman here is Uncle Steve."

"What's your name?" asked Uncle Steve, an old man with a gleaming dental plate that seemed to be giving him the same kind of trouble that bits give horses, and that produced a sound like a child's rattle whenever he spoke.

"I can cook," Mary said calmly after a while, scrutinizing the two gentlemen, to their evident displeasure. From time to time bleary-eyed Uncle Delbert would take the pince-nez off his nose and dry the lenses with a piece of cloth.

"Goodness, child, no one expects such things of you—I mean that you should cook," Uncle Steve said with a smile that one might—in biblical terminology—characterize as wicked. "Why should such a beautiful girl cook at all?"

"How about telling us your name?" Uncle Delbert inquired again. His hairless scalp gleamed as if treated with furniture polish, one of the great innovations of those years. The gentleman named Delbert also had teeth, Mary noticed, but his were more like piano keys, some raised and others depressed.

This time Uncle Delbert's voice took on a more commanding tone—and a convincing one at that, for just fifteen years ago he had stood at the helm of a large enterprise. "All right now, what's your name?"

"Mary."

"Mary? Mary? Mary!" cried the uncle who called himself Delbert, while the uncle who called himself

Steve was convulsed with both laughter and delight. "Mary!"

"*Our* Mary!" They kept exclaiming it over and over, limply slapping their thighs. "*Our* Mary!"

Mary had no idea why her name so tickled these two old men to a near-agony of amusement, though she guessed they must be thinking of somebody else. That somebody (for the reader's information) was Mary Anderson, the most celebrated actress in New York, an ideal of feminine beauty whose fans liked to call her, simply: "*Our* Mary!"

They finally stopped laughing, exhausted and out of breath, shaking their heads over the miracle of coincidence: "*Our* Mary has come!"

Uncle Delbert, who was perhaps the younger of the two, gradually recovered from his joy and suddenly grabbed his chest with such brusqueness it seemed he might be suffering a stroke. Then he pulled out a wallet, seized a few of the green bills with quivering fingers, and held them out to Mary. "Here," he said, "this is yours." He came closer to Mary, puckered his lips in preparation for a fatherly kiss, and abruptly started back.

"What happened?" asked Uncle Steve, alarmed.

"You came off an immigrant ship, right?" asked Uncle Delbert. "From where? It isn't Poland, is it?"

"Who cares?" Uncle Steve interjected soothingly.

"Well, *I* certainly care," snapped Uncle Delbert, quivering with rage. "Out with it now, an immigrant ship or Poland, which is it? Immigrants stink for months, Polacks even longer. I know the smell. You don't spend your life in the shipping business for nothing."

"Why don't you just forget about it, good friend," the other man suggested, still trying to calm Uncle Delbert. "Look now, isn't this a beautiful child? Just look at those bright eyes. Come closer to the fireplace, come!"

Mary disengaged herself from his hands, took the bank notes to the couch, and concealed them in her basket. Then she returned.

"OK," Uncle Delbert said with his commanding voice, "and now you take off your skirt and your bloomers."

Mary obeyed like a windup doll or like any child carelessly taking off her clothes.

"Easy, easy," whispered Uncle Steve. "Not too hasty."

"Slower, much slower," added the other uncle.

"Now turn around, like that. There!"

"Uncle Steve is a doctor, he'll give you a checkup, all right? There's nothing to be afraid of."

Doctor? Mary gave a start.

"But no! Why should anyone be afraid of a doctor? Come!"

The two gentlemen touched and palpated her, turned her bare buttocks toward the fireplace, and watched with ancient childish eyes how the tender flesh gradually took on a reddish glow.

"Divine," one of them whispered, while the other, who was something of an art connoisseur, added amid heavy breathing: "Rubenesque."

"If only she were three or four years older," Uncle Delbert whispered, "she'd catch fire herself. I've seen lust like that in my day."

"Well," said Uncle Steve, "I bet it's been a long time since you've been able to put out *that* kind of fire."

This sparked a violent quarrel between the two, so that they stood shouting and fulminating at each other—without, however, taking their eyes off the girl and her backside. Then the man in livery stepped in, unbidden

54

and unannounced, and asked the gentlemen for permission to take the little miss to her room.

"But certainly, Ferguson," said Uncle Steve, "remove the child from the sight of that old swine over there. Don't you agree, Delbert, dear uncle?"

Mary got dressed, took her basket, and followed the man in livery to a room with a freshly made bed. He would give her Uncle Delbert's address in the morning, he said. Uncle Delbert was a lawyer who lived on Gramercy Park, and his wife just happened to be looking for a maid. Mary might do well to introduce herself—with the necessary discretion, of course.

Mary had never heard the word "discretion" before today, but she assumed it was something to be on one's guard against.

15

The next morning Mary was on her way to Gramercy Park. Mrs. Delbert Scott herself opened the door and immediately apologized: her maid had rudely left her in the lurch three days ago. She sighed. But as she spoke, she noticed that the girl facing her was not at all suitably attired; in fact, she was shabbily dressed, and shabby clothes were by definition dirty. Mrs. Scott's tone of voice became cool and disdainful. Was the girl here to ask for a handout, she inquired.

Not at all—Mary tried to explain that she was looking for a position as a household helper. "I can cook." She rattled off a few more sentences she had prepared and memorized. Another fine lady, she said, a lady

56

whose name she couldn't remember at the moment, had given her the address.

"Oh!" Mrs. Delbert Scott motioned her into the house with a condescending gesture and led her into the kitchen, where Mrs. Scott sat down and let Mary remain standing. Since Mrs. Delbert Scott was a chatterbox that had been unable to spill out its contents for days, Mary's company wasn't altogether unwelcome. On the contrary, the more she talked (fingering her pearl necklace like a rosary), indeed the more attentively Mary seemed to be listening, the greater was Mrs. Scott's goodwill toward this girl who claimed to have worked for a family in Boston. After twenty minutes of uninterrupted speech on her part and near silence on Mary's, Mrs. Scott decided that this young girl must be quite exceptionally intelligent.

She also told Mary a few things about the master of the house. Delbert L. Scott was plagued by all sorts of allergies and had to spend days in a row at the sulfur baths. Afterward he'd feel such an itch to get back to work—"and just imagine, he's in his late seventies!" —that he'd occasionally spend the night at the office. She, for her part, had been subject to attacks of depression ever since a female cousin from her mother's side of the family had drowned in a small Canadian lake. Presumably it had been either an Indian or a treacherous whirlpool that had dragged her into the depths; at any rate, they never found her body . . .

Mary was wondering whether corpses could really just vanish like that, whether the Indians—, but Mrs. Scott concluded her thoughts and announced that she had made up her mind to hire Mary, at least on probation. Just a little meat, lots of vegetables and salads, yes, she was feeling more and more drawn to vegetarianism, and on Fridays, when she recuperated by staying in bed and fasting, just one cup of tea would do.

Whereupon she showed Mary the maid's room and urgently requested that she not go to the bathroom at night, if at all possible, since Mrs. Scott was frightened to death at the mere thought of burglars.

For supper that evening Mrs. Scott requested a light vegetable soup, a glass of goat's milk, and some lettuce.

And Mr. Scott?

Mr. Scott had gone to visit some friends in the country, all passionate bridge players.

The next morning Mrs. Scott introduced the new domestic to Mr. Delbert L. Scott, and the way the old gentleman greeted Mary, they might have been as unacquainted with each other as a Kentucky hillbilly and the Paris Obelisk. For the rest, though, he proved extremely pleasant, and after a few days Mary began to suspect that he didn't remember her face at all, that there was no room left in his brain for anything but the flame-reddened cheeks of young girls' behinds. Still, from time to time, very secretively, he would stuff a few dollar bills into Mary's apron pocket, but without so much as a conspiratorial wink of an eye.

Three weeks later, Delbert L. Scott was a widower. The sickness was diagnosed as typhus—*Typhus abdominalis*—by none other than Uncle Dr. Steve. Mrs. Delbert had not suffered a great deal, "she just passed away," as Mr. Scott put it. In the smoking room the two gentlemen partook of another two or three Cognacs, and Uncle Steve scribbled his signature on the death certificate.

16

Two days after Mrs. Delbert Scott's death, the house was black with mourners. Mr. Scott had asked the undertaker to organize and conduct the obsequies, including the reception afterward, and so the employees of Hoobe's funeral home walked about serving drinks with their deadpan expressions, looking like obsequious corpses.

Mary hid in her room, keeping the door slightly open in case she was still needed. The discreet murmuring of conversation gradually yielded to noisier talk, some stifled snickers followed, and finally something very much like gaiety filled the house. Mrs. Delbert Scott—whose own first name was known only to her most intimate lady friends—had left behind an explicit clause in her will, stating that she, who had always been so sad,

59

wanted everyone to celebrate her arrival at the feet of the Almighty—immediately, if at all possible. "Yes, make a joyful noise!"

Later the hearse drove off, drawn by black horses and followed by hundreds of horse-drawn buggies, so that the whole street resounded with the noise of hooves. The silence that then set in prompted Mary to cautiously open the door, until finally, slowly, with hesitant steps, she walked down the stairs.

What she found there can only be called a scene of devastation, but of a sort she had not encountered before—an elegant sort: empty glasses, some of them tipped over; plates, some of them broken, laden with partially eaten sandwiches; damask napkins bunched up and tossed aside; Havana cigars lit, briefly puffed on, then crushed in an ashtray; little heaps of confectioner's sugar on the tablecloths; an open Bible stained with wine; ladies' hats with black mourning bands; a man's scarf rolled up, concealing a card with a lady's address; asparagus tips trampled into the rug; a half-eaten pear. Even the framed mirrors were a mess, as if some ladies had been overcome by self-hate in the midst of putting on makeup and spat at their images in the mirror.

As she stood contemplating this scene, a young man with a scarf wrapped around his chin and mouth stepped out of a corner. He had a pistol in his hand. Mary let out a scream.

The presumable robber kept his hand pressed over her mouth long enough for her to notice (though she was close to suffocation) that he himself was quivering from head to toe.

His name was Chris Cramer.

17

These were the years when
people still read Horatio Alger, Jr. His books outsold
Mark Twain and sometimes even the Bible. His heroes—
but only the heroes—were magnanimous and decent to
a degree that was almost indecent. One truism applied
to all his characters: the girls became women but the
boys remained boys. As a one-time Sunday-school teacher
of little boys, Horatio Alger, Jr., had occasionally guided
some of his flock off the straight and narrow and into
the bushes, and for this he was very nearly hanged from
a branch by a mob of decent people from whom he
escaped with a last-minute leap onto the last running
board of a railroad train. He settled down in New York
and there plied the writer's trade, continuing to minis-
ter to the needs of boys—their moral needs, this time.

He wrote countless books in which boys could find foolproof recipes for success, all nicely wrapped up in a gripping adventure story. He remained otherwise helpful, too, but that he is so ignored today (his books withdrawn from libraries for lack of interest) proves, I believe, that virtue is only one of the many spices of art.

Chris Cramer, the burglar, having been whipped out of house and home by his father, a ceaselessly drunk tinsmith, had come to New York from Kansas City two years before. He had worked as a wheel-joint oiler. He had not spent his spare time with girls, beer, or loafing; no, he had read. Sometimes after a train pulled in at Grand Central Depot, he had had to clean the cars. One day he found a booklet about Mark, the young match vendor. This hero ignited Chris Cramer's soul. He began to read Horatio Alger's books and pamphlets like a man possessed; he would have stolen them if he hadn't gotten to know several conversion-hungry moralists who gave them away for free. The author preached virtue, abstinence, honesty, and especially politeness. It was better, according to him, to greet someone once too often than once too little, for you could never tell whether it might not be someone important whose feelings you were hurting. Let's say a coin accidentally drops out of an elderly gentleman's pocket: you should immediately bend down and return it to him. The man might be an Astor or a Rockefeller and feel so touched he offers you an important position. Politeness to old ladies might also result in their virtually throwing you upstairs.

In reality things looked different. Once, Chris Cramer had rescued a child from the wheels of a carriage whose horses had bolted. The child's father *looked* like a millionaire, but he gave Chris Cramer a slap in the face for being rude. Another time Chris Cramer actually saw

63

a wallet falling out of a gentleman's coat, but no sooner had he bent down to pick it up than the man seized him in the act of exercising his virtue, called a policeman, and accused his benefactor of theft. Fortunately, the cop was drunk and made do with a few hefty blows of his truncheon. Another time in the park he had come upon a man of sterling appearance who had inexplicably sunk into a swoon onto a park bench; when he called an ambulance, the gentleman woke up and accused him of stealing his gold watch. And there was another time when, at considerable risk to his own health, he had saved a somewhat inebriated financier from a ballroom battle and was punished with a merciless caning for having prevented the gentleman from experiencing a real brawl. Yes, and once he had helped a lady carry her valise to her house; she invited him to tea and cake, took to fumbling at his belt buckle, and when, disappointed, he bade her farewell, she screamed out the window: "Rape! Rape! Rape!" That alone cost him eight months in juvenile detention.

Virtue had not paid, not even once, and it was the rich—the second string, so to speak, among Horatio Alger's heroes—who were the worst of all.

Gradually there developed and hardened in Chris Cramer's mind the conviction that some rich people weren't really worthy of their wealth and didn't give a rat's tail for the virtue of the poor. He even began to suspect that the rich weren't really interested in making the poor a little less poor. This insight tipped the balance. Though he was much too kind to be a criminal, he decided to embark upon a career of moderate crime. Having gotten to know the power of the rich, he restricted his legal transgressions to members of the middle class.

This led to a second moral crisis. Nineteen percent

of the city's population were rich or well-to-do, while 72 percent were poor, which meant he had to restrict his burglaries to the remaining 9 percent, the middle class. This further insight prompted him to return to work at the depot for two months, till he regained the necessary inner balance.

His specialty—though he did not really have a great deal of experience yet—was breaking into a well-to-do home immediately after someone died there, since usually the whole household, servants and all, went to the cemetery. He kept track of obituary notices in the *Herald Tribune*.

Mary learned these things on the very first evening, and to tell the truth, she was offended.

"That's the way life is," he said at the end, and then he asked her a question: "Can you steal?"

She shook her head. She couldn't do anything much except cook.

She liked the young man.

18

Chris Cramer forbade Mary to clean up the debris of the mourning party; he told her to fetch her belongings and leave with him. He himself used the brief wait to gather together a few objects that could be easily hidden in his pockets and under his coat.

Chris Cramer was twenty-three years old, a colossus with a child's face. Staring out from under his bulging forehead was a sinister pair of eyes; but maybe they just looked that way since his brows were contracted as if in constant effort. He had huge hands with dimples above the knuckles, and long, corkscrew locks of blond hair. The only thing that really mattered to Mary was this: Chris Cramer reminded her of Sean Mallon, the cook, her constant companion during most of that horrible voyage aboard the *Leibnitz*.

"I think so," Mary said when Chris Cramer asked her on that first evening in his shack whether she was still a virgin, adding that he didn't really care one way or the other.

He had stuck four apples on a spit and was now cutting thin slices off a bacon rind, wrapping them around the apples and fastening them with tiny nails. "Make sure you don't forget the nails," he said, "it's just like watching for bones in fish."

He set fire to a heap of box boards in the fireplace, covered the flames with sawed-off branches, and soon built up a steady blaze. Wood wasn't hard to come by; there was plenty of it right around the corner, scattered about like driftwood on a beach. He coughed. "The flue's no good," he said.

He wiped his hands dry. Did she like his place—aside from the smoke?

Mary nodded enthusiastically. It was a strange place to live in. Chris Cramer had tacked up on the walls countless scraps of cloth: segments of gowns, shirts, trousers, and overcoats, strips and rags of all colors, including white and black: as if, without being very meticulous, he wished to perpetuate the tradition of patchwork and quilt he had grown up with in the Midwest. After a pause he asked what part of the world *she* came from.

"Ireland," she answered, without hesitation. Immediately he laughed and took to mimicking her unmistakably Swiss-German accent. He could spot an Irish accent as well, he pointed out—and even the most backwoodsy Irish folk spoke better English than she.

Mary said nothing. She was not about to give up her invented identity.

"Let's eat," he suggested. "Want some bread?" She nodded. He cut two pieces, letting the slices drop on the table.

Mary, indignant, searched for a formulation that would be both brief and not give away her secret.

"Bread comes from God," she said.

"Yes," he replied, unmoved. "So does roast pig."

He pulled the steaming apples off the spit, wrapped them in a piece of newspaper, and put them on the table, carefully this time. "Help yourself!"

She obeyed.

"So your name's Mary. Mary who?"

"Mary. Mary Mallon."

He looked at her quizzically, then nodded and said: "All right, have it your way. Mary Mallon."

He cautiously bit off a piece of hot apple. "Sleepy?" he asked. She nodded.

"Go on and lie down. There're two mattresses in the corner. Pick one for yourself."

Chris Cramer still sat facing the fireplace and didn't notice Mary was beginning to take off her clothes, slowly but without hesitation; and when he inadvertently turned and saw her half naked, he ordered her not to undress any further. He did not sound upset, only determined.

He stood up, wrapped her in the blanket like a small child, and laid her down on one of the mattresses. "Tomorrow we'll talk about your future." Mary wanted to interrupt him, but he put two fingers over her lips and continued: "Yes, of course you can cook! Go to sleep now!"

Chris Cramer tried to sleep as well; and then, without actually taking aim, he threw a shoe at a rat lurking nearby. He slept, woke up again, tried to pray several times, and gave up, distracted by other thoughts. Prayer wasn't really worth a damn, since if God was thinking about something himself, how could he pay attention to people's thoughts?

Mary woke up at dawn and watched the rats. She had gotten so used to rats on the *Leibnitz* that they seemed like domesticated animals to her.

19

The area I live in—Riverside Drive, on the Upper West Side—is what's called a "transitional area." A lot of Hitler refugees live here, along with their children and grandchildren. Caucasian white blends into Puerto Rican tan, then darkens around 125th Street into black combined with garish, not always tasteful attire. But isn't it in poor taste for a man in my condition to think about something as trivial as taste? Strange to think that ninety years ago Riverside Drive was almost uninhabited—hills sparsely covered with trees and grass. But little more than an hour's walk away, in downtown Manhattan, were factories where according to present-day estimates more than a hundred thousand children were put to work for as long as ten hours a day, under backbreaking conditions and for less than a pittance.

Chris Cramer lived on Water Street, in a wooden shack he had hammered together on the foundations of a burned-down house that had been built in Dutch style. The cracks were insulated with starchpaste and manure. There were no windows; the whole thing had been built for protection against the cold winter, and during the summer he slept on the roof. He was proud of this house, especially the inside.

Mary, pretending to be asleep, peeked out from under the pillow and watched him washing himself and getting dressed; indeed she admired him, admired everything he did.

He scribbled a few lines on a scrap of paper; then he seemed to ponder whether Mary could read and write; he shrugged and walked out. Mary got up quickly and read the note. It said he had some business to take care of on Mercer Street, there was tea on the shelf and a few things to eat, and he was leaving half a dollar in case there was something she needed urgently.

Mary got dressed. Now that the odor of woodsmoke had dissipated, there were peculiar smells in the house. In one corner it was the smell of cheap perfume that rose to her nostrils; other places emitted rancid or sour smells, poor smells or sweet smells—dampness and age, that incense of poverty she knew all too well. The more pleasant smells arose from clothes that had once been worn by the better sort of people.

Chris Cramer's hammer-and-nails work had proved incomparable as far as sheer diligence went. Mary opened the door of the room (which was also the door of the house) and put a brick between the threshold and the door. In a little while fresh air came in, along with an icy draft.

She discovered several heaps of Horatio Alger novels. As she began to stack them up, she came across a good dozen empty wallets, some of them monogrammed. One or two contained calling cards. Ladies' purses, too, and some fine silk kerchiefs. She already knew Chris Cramer was a thief, but now she was afraid. She hastily wrapped the stuff in newspaper, ran two blocks down the street, dumped the package in a doorway, and returned out of breath. She decided to clean the floor. It reminded her of the bar in port where she had sat waiting to board the *Leibnitz*. Swarms of vermin were breeding beneath pamphlets and newspapers. She scrubbed the floor and washed the furniture (fragments of furniture, actually), and wondered whether she shouldn't write a love letter to Chris Cramer. But she dropped the idea, since she didn't know what exactly you were supposed to say in a love letter.

When Chris Cramer came home several hours later, she didn't return his hello but instead immediately started telling him about the wallets she'd found. She begged him to promise her never, never to steal again. He just laughed and said that if he stopped stealing they'd both starve.

"Bullshit," said Mary, proud of the word. Once she'd found a job as a cook, he wouldn't have to steal: "I'm a cook." And to prove to him what she could do and how seriously she took it, she asked him to get a pencil and paper. Then, in her clumsy English, she dictated her first recipe, for oxtail soup.

20

Cut up an oxtail with a chopping knife; this won't be hard, since the tail has joints for moving easily, since oxes, who don't get milked, like to swing this part of their body back and forth or lift it for certain reasons (cow dung). Each piece of tail is a little bit fatty on top. Braise them with oil or lard in a frying pan until they start to turn brown. But you'll need the following additions too, and these should be cut into very small pieces before braising the meat: two pounds carrots for eight people, one pound leeks, nine medium onions, one pound celery, one pound cabbage. Also salt, pepper, garlic. Now pour two quarts of water over the braised oxtail parts and boil for at least two hours. Let the whole thing cool enough for you to take the meat off the bones without burning your fingers.

The bones can be thrown to stray dogs or given to beggars you know and like." (This sentence was Chris Cramer's.) "Tear the meat itself into small pieces with your fingertips; this is a boring job, so roll up your sleeves when you do it. Take the little pieces and put them back in the broth, this time in a large pot. Now simmer the meat and vegetables for an hour. Shortly before the sixty minutes have passed, pour some oil in a frying pan, add flour, and push the flour back and forth until it turns brown, almost black, and then add this to the oxtail soup, which will make a loud hissing sound as you put it in, because oil can get hotter than water. The burned flour makes for a slightly bitter taste, but you can correct this with a little Madeira or a spoonful of sugar just before serving. People who know a lot about oxtail soup often spice it with chives or parsley."

The process of writing down this recipe took almost as much time as it takes to cook oxtail soup, and Chris Cramer's wrist ached, for he was not a writer like Horatio Alger, Jr., who must have had wrists of steel to write as much as he did—and from this Chris Cramer concluded that mental work demanded a considerable amount of physical strength. Once again he kept his lips pressed tight together so as not to reveal how greatly he longed to write books of his own someday.

The next morning, on the way to the library, Chris

Cramer ran into Al Fogerty, a fellow he didn't particularly like, mainly because he was a braggart and had a way of physically forcing himself on whoever he happened to be talking to, so that you had to step backward again and again just to keep your distance from him. Chris Cramer tried to hurry on, but Fogerty grabbed him by the sleeve.

"What's the matter," he said, "don't you know your friends anymore?"

A pretty cheeky remark, considering it was Chris Cramer who had once wangled the police off Fogerty's scent.

Al Fogerty was smartly dressed; he seemed to have come up in the world. As it turned out, he had recently landed a job as doorman at the St. Denis Hotel. He boasted and told stories about famous people most folks knew only from the papers. Unfortunately, he had no more time to lose, he had to get moving. But if he could help Chris Cramer in any way . . . Chris didn't believe a word; still, he asked whether Al could help get someone a job in the hotel. Why, certainly, he said; was Chris still at his old place? Good, he'd drop by that very evening.

If that happened, it would be worth a letter to Horatio Alger, thought Chris Cramer: a man himself barely out of the gutter helping you out!

But that very evening, Al Fogerty knocked on the door and stepped in.

"You helped me," Al Fogerty said, "and looking around this hole, it seems to me you could use a little help as well."

Al was not ashamed to make a display of disgust at the destitution evident in his friend's living quarters: he turned up his nose and began to scratch himself as if an army of lice were already climbing up his calves. Just then, as he stood there wordlessly scratching himself, Mary returned, coat in hand and swinging a basket full of fruit and vegetables. She went up to Chris and kissed him—the way a child kisses an adult, but it still embarrassed him—and threw her coat on the bed. She was wearing a light blue polka-dot dress with cup-shaped lace frills at the sleeves and collar.

"Do you like it?" she asked, disregarding Al Fogerty. Chris didn't even seem to notice the dress; he was closely observing the lecherous look in Fogerty's eyes. Fogerty, who'd seen many fine ladies and gentlemen at his hotel, tried to kiss the back of Mary's hand. She pulled it away from him, almost disgusted by the gesture, and still her eyes seemed to hope for a compliment from Chris Cramer.

"This is my friend Al Fogerty," he said, and explained the background.

"I'll certainly help," Al exclaimed.

Chris ignored him and talked about finding work for Mary at the St. Denis, as a chambermaid or ironing woman or whatever. Mary interrupted him, annoyed he had said not a word about her cooking ability.

Al nodded and said he personally didn't doubt her ability in the slightest, but that no first-rate hotel restaurant would hire a female cook, only female assistants, and that this amounted to little more than peeling potatoes; however, thanks to his special relationship with the chef, a certain Jules d'Albert, probably he, Al Fogerty, could find her a better job in the kitchen. M. d'Albert came from Paris and was really a very understanding person.

Perhaps he noticed how little understanding Mary had for the many understanding people whose paths had crossed hers, for she didn't smile until Al Fogerty went on to say that the food at the St. Denis was so extraordinary that those who dined there would some-times sneak off to the powder room and stick a finger down their throat, just so they could keep on indulging. He would return with a definite report within twenty-four hours, said Al Fogerty. He put on the buckskin gloves an Englishman had left lying by the desk, bowed, and walked out of the shack. Chris threw a shoe after him, as he would at a rat.

Mary began to clean up. She dreamed of hotel kit-chens where she would walk to and fro someday, tast-ing this, testing that. She would have boletus mushrooms shipped from back home, where they came shooting up wherever you looked in the summer and early fall when Holymarymotherofgod had cried tears of rain and the wind came following after.

"What the hell's going on?" Chris Cramer asked, throwing the second shoe, and Mary said she was so happy, all she wanted now was to be Chris Cramer's wife and then everything would be good.

"Nothing will be good," said Chris Cramer. "This is not time to start a family and have children, and cer-tainly not with a silly goose who doesn't even have real pubic hair yet." He went to the fireplace and rekindled the fire with the bellows. He started undressing. Mary watched the broad-shouldered but—as she realized only now—terribly thin man, watched him with love and pity. Chris Cramer told her she'd better close her eyes and lie down on her side with her face turned away, or she'd get a thrashing. Mary obeyed.

The next morning during breakfast he explained that she was welcome to live with him as a daughter or sister, but that she should not count on his loving her. "What should I do then?" she asked. Before anything else she should learn to speak decent English, he replied, or she'd always end up the sucker. She should spend time at the markets, get to know them, the Fulton market, or Paddy's market, or Union market by the East River; the city was full of markets, and if she wanted to earn money she'd be sure to find an odd job at one of these markets, especially the ones where German immigrants set up stalls. And he, Chris Cramer, would take care of her as long as she did what he told her to do, and as for himself, he'd take care of his own business just fine without her advice. Besides, he'd decided to join a 'forbidden anarchist party. Someday he'd explain to her what anarchism was all about, but for the time being she was too dumb.

The women Mary bought groceries from were of German stock. Mary watched how they pressed down the scale pan to increase the weight, and how they put fresh fruit on top of the rotten stuff; how, under cover of friendly chatter and concerned inquiries about the health of the customer's family, they'd pinch a few coins from the change they were handing over.

21

One morning a messenger knocked on the door and delivered a card. Al Fogerty had not been bluffing. Monsieur Jules d'Albert was, in two tersely worded lines, inviting Mary to an interview at the hotel, at 3:30 P.M. Immediately Mary began to wash herself, to comb her hair and get dressed. She moved as quietly as she could, though she guessed that Chris was only pretending to be asleep. She took all the time she needed to make herself pretty—powdering her cheeks (she wasn't quite expert at this yet), smoothing down her eyebrows with a little glue, and rubbing lavender perfume into her skin. Examining herself in the mirror, she noticed with pleasure how much older she looked with makeup. She slipped into her new dress and, with one remarkably nimble motion, gathered and pinned up her blond hair into a coil, leaving out a few tousled curls.

It was April weather outside, alternating sunshine and showers, so she decided to spend the next few hours under a roof. She stuffed pencil and writing paper into her pocketbook, plus a few dollars she still had left over, and took a coach to Trinity Church—that way neither dress nor boots could get dirty. She curtsied, knelt down for a moment in God's house, crossed herself, then sat in one of the front pews. She worshipped Jesus, but felt no love for Him; in fact, this was the first time she had thought about Him in months. She wondered what kind of job He would have had in this city, and whether He would have managed to find twelve men to follow Him. And why didn't He convert more than a couple of women, and those more or less in passing? Why weren't there any women among His disciples? Was He anything like Chris Cramer, physically? And why didn't He ever talk about cooking, only about feeding the four thousand? Was He a vegetarian? Who could have prepared lamb more deliciously than He? Why did Chris never speak of Him, and how would Jesus have judged Chris? Would He have blessed him for his continence? If not, why hadn't He made him potent?

Thus she sat for hours. Once in a while people would come into the church, pray, and usually leave in a hurry. She wanted to write a letter to her relatives in Rhäzüns, searched for her pencil, and found among various other papers a sheet that had been folded several times. It was the list of foodstuffs the emigration authorities in Germany had recommended for the trip across the sea: "40 lbs. biscuits, 170 lbs. potatoes, 5 lbs. flour, 6 lbs. ham, 2 lbs. salt," and last but not least, "2 bottles olive oil, onions, and pepper," for (so it said on the paper) there was nothing better for a seasick stomach than potato salad. Someone else had suggested twenty eggs per person, plus lots of dried fruit. A second list "urgently" recommended "blankets, sheets, 1 plate, 1 cup, 1 spoon, 1 fork, 1 chamber pot."

Overwhelmed by homesickness, she began to cry; and after a while she started writing a letter to her relatives. But there was something in the way. She would have to tell what had happened to her parents and sisters, and she didn't want to hurt those she'd left behind. And here she was dreaming the time away—was it three already? She quickly put pencil and paper back into her purse. She hailed a coach and asked the driver to stop a block from the hotel entrance; something told her a hotel would not like its employees, even future employees, stepping from a coach at the main entrance. She lifted her skirt and tried to walk on tiptoe. A slushy snow was falling.

Al Fogerty saw her coming. Nearly frozen to the bone, he rushed out of his booth—no, no, she wasn't late at all. Mary interrupted him with a gesture of disregard, and before she could even say the name "Jules d'Albert," the man himself appeared in the main entrance, perhaps by chance and perhaps not, and sent Al Fogerty away.

By the standards of the era M. Jules d'Albert was a handsome man: short, tough, and suave, with a pointed, prominent chin and feminine cheeks. A look of humble lechery lurked in his eyes; his dark hair was greased and slicked back. After the obligatory bow came a handshake like the grip of a steel clamp, an introduction of sorts: it said, more directly than words could have, that she was a hireling, a future subordinate, who needn't try to divine her proper place in the hierarchy of employees. His glance quickly appraised her figure and returned to her face. He seemed to like what he saw. He gave a bellboy instructions to wait with Mary for two minutes and then lead her to his private suite.

The bellboy appeared to be silently counting sixty seconds twice over; as soon as the time was up, his neck leaped from his collar like a cuckoo bird from its clock. She followed him up three flights of stairs, disappointed that she hadn't been taken up in an elevator. But to prevent the disgruntlement from spoiling her demeanor, she conjured up a look of indifference, something she'd practiced in church. The bellboy bowed in front of an unnumbered door, knocked twice, and hurried away. A muffled voice asked her in. She remained stubbornly standing in front of the door until M. d'Albert himself finally opened it with an annoyed look on his face.

22

Of course, he gallantly helped her out of her coat. Then he assumed a stern and fatherly air and sat down, leaving Mary standing. He let his fingers playfully run through the velvet cord fringes of a sofa and gradually talked himself into the role of sympathetic *chef de cuisine* wishing nothing more than to convey certain matters of policy and basic principle. He asked whether Mary had ever heard of a third-class, let alone second-class, restaurant with a female cook. He wouldn't even mention first-class restaurants; hell would freeze over before they'd let a woman do their cooking. Mary obediently shook her head. Undoubtedly within a few years Mary could find a job as private cook in a decent household—she was still young, surely no more than eighteen—providing, of course, she show a tireless willingness to learn and an equally tireless willingness to work. There was absolutely no conflict between the two; on the contrary, a good worker should consider it his obligation to perform additional services another employee might have overlooked, there was even a Latin proverb concerning these things, and—apropos— did Mary speak Latin with any fluency? She shook her head, but noticed that M. d'Albert occasionally forgot his French accent and spoke just as vulgarly as most people she'd come across. He seemed to have noticed this, for at that moment he recovered his nasal accent and delivered a new sermon on obedience and a good employee's readiness to oblige; why, Hannibal himself had written about these things in detail a long time ago, and how else could he have crossed the Alps with three hundred elephants? Did Mary know the Alps? She shook her head uncertainly, and d'Albert stood up and disappeared behind a screen, to get into something more comfortable, he said. Mary noticed there were pictures of Chinese people painted on the screen.

She shyly looked around M. d'Albert's suite. There was a little table made completely of marble, and on this table stood a chessboard made of light and dark green marble. There were pink Ionic pillars, Persian rugs from Hoboken, massive dark pieces of oak furniture, and hanging over all these *objets* a chandelier with crystal droplets so genteel they tinkled if you just yawned. What interested Mary most was a birdless birdcage made of polished brass.

M. d'Albert came out from behind the screen, stark naked, delicately virile, and teasingly beckoned Mary with a summoning finger, and, somewhat more commandingly, with the lower body's important index finger. She understood and began to strip off her clothes, not at all coyly but rather as if dress and petticoat were a

85

sort of encumbering gift wrap. M. d'Albert nodded and smiled at his ability to issue silent commands. But then he took pleasure in her firm flesh and youthful skin. As he finally started steering his way toward climax, he cried: "Maria . . . Madonna . . . Maria . . .", and from this Mary concluded that at least the mother of her bedmate was not French but Italian, maybe from Hoboken, like his Persian carpets.

After recovering from his exhaustion, M. d'Albert promised that one of these days he would dictate a particularly subtle French recipe to her, a recipe to be found in only one place outside his own brain, and that was the safe deposit vault of a bank in Boston. Mary did not listen, but cuddled up against him. She was pleased with the good start things had taken and was speculating whether M. d'Albert might not even make a decent spouse, with her as his fellow spouse in the kitchen. She drew the practical consequences of this new perspective and immediately began to caress his midsection. He, however, was tired, jammed his elbow untenderly into her ribs, and informed her of the hour she should show up for work in the kitchen the next morning.

Mary got dressed and left.

23

Jules d'Albert was a swine, and Mary promptly found out how far-reaching were the practical implications of his introductory lecture. He had her peel potatoes, cut onions, wash lettuce, until her hands, which were certainly used to hard work, puffed up and turned a dark red. This did not deter him from leading her into the cellar during her half-hour break and taking his pleasure with rabbitlike haste, after removing her underwear with a single swift one-handed maneuver. When he finished he'd give her a pat on the behind and send her upstairs. The other women in the kitchen would welcome her back with malicious smirks, for they weren't any better off. Every kitchen assistant had her own *jour fixe* in the cellar, and just like Mary, none of them had seen M. d'Albert's suite more than once.

The noise and heat didn't take getting used to; Mary had already experienced the atmosphere of a big kitchen during her weeks on the *Leibnitz*. But there was more shouting here than on the ship, where just three people had done all the work. Here plates and potlids rattled and clattered; furious waiters came storming back with meals rejected by fastidious or squeamish guests.

At four-thirty Mary was allowed to go home, tired but happy. She saw herself closer to her distant professional goal. Sometimes in the evenings she felt she ought to give Chris some consolation, he spoke so often and with a bad conscience about how real anarchists were too busy to hold a regular job. He read and read, and the books piled up around his mattress. He knew a group of people, immigrants mostly, who supplied him with reading matter.

Mary's expectations were badly disappointed when she received her wages at the end of the week. One of her friendlier fellow workers explained that you had to compensate by helping yourself to groceries and hiding them under your skirt, that no one would miss them anyway. This was true, for M. d'Albert had calculated theft into his budget.

Two months went by in this manner, days of hard work and happy evenings with Chris Cramer, who occasionally read her something he thought she would like; until one morning Mary arrived in the hotel kitchen and was told that she'd have to work extra hard that day because three assistants and one cook were seriously ill. It was M. d'Albert who informed her of this. Mary was seized by an anxiety she herself could not explain, as though something were telling her to flee. She decided instead to stay.

The following morning two more cooks failed to show up, as well as a fourth assistant (there were seven altogether). One of the waiters hadn't shown up for work, either. No cause for alarm, in M. d'Albert's opinion. He sent an immediate notice of dismissal to each of his sick employees and hired a few unemployed loiterers off the street to replace the assistants. You're here to work, not to beg! The *chef de cuisine* did what he could to knock this truth into their heads: he worked them twice as hard as regular employees and paid half their salary.

In a week the St. Denis Hotel had to close down. Among those who'd become ill were two gentlemen who'd had a business lunch at the hotel and were well known throughout the city; they had notified the editors of several newspapers as soon as their first aches and pains set in, for their symptoms were identical. The editors concurred that one rich man may suffer misfortune at the hands of the world, but not two at the same time in the same place. Since the two gentlemen had lived long past their sturdiest years (spent "betting on fast women and slow horses"), and since they were overfed besides, it took only a short time for both to find heaven's mercy and a sumptuous burial. The newspapers screamed themselves hoarse: "Mr. Stewart Carter is dead! Mr. Everett Douglas is dead! St. Denis Hotel! Plague! Plague! Plague!"

M. d'Albert gave the kitchen personnel their severance pay—seven dollars for assistants, ten for cooks. But then something unexpected happened. While the cooks and girls apathetically accepted their pittance, Mary kept in the background, malice in her pale eyes, and didn't approach her boss until the others had left. Her demands weren't the least bit dainty. Not only did she insist he hand over three times the amount he was offering—lest she pay a visit to the newspapers and let them know about certain working conditions—she went so far as to dictate to him a first-rate letter of recommendation, a virtual pedigree of gastronomic mastery. M. d'Albert did not hesitate for a moment (sometimes even meanness has style): he gave her the money, he wrote the letter, and when he bade her farewell he smiled and even bowed to her.

Working for M. d'Albert had been a gain for Mary in every respect. She had always brought pencil and paper and taken notes on how to spice meat, fish, and vegetables; the decorative patterns of delicate tidbits spread on silver and porcelain platters were imprinted in her memory. Now her dainty nose could distinguish with seismographic precision which color (of a sauce, for example) would harmonize with which odor; at the same time she had learned to despise those supremely refined concoctions, confidence tricks on the palate, that hardly deserved to be called food anymore. She wanted to cook for people who liked to eat, not just prove how much money they had. They'd have to be high-class folk, to be sure, not your ordinary soup-kitchen sort. She decided definitely for coarse-grain bread as against white rolls, for pure fruit over fruit in syrup.

I as her chronicler can only agree with her. "With good bread the coarsest fare is tolerable; without it, the most luxurious table is not comfortable." Thus wrote a certain Mary Cornelius in 1845, a quarter of a century before Mary Mallon, in her cookbook, *The Young Housekeeper's Friend*.

Talent is as talent does—it takes intuitive possession of what others have already accomplished and simultaneously ventures forth into uncharted land. Mary, of course, had her own way of doing that, and her fantastic talent confined itself to soups, roasts, vegetables, breads, salads, and desserts. After love, food is the most important thing in life, and whoever thinks politics more important should ponder the fact that politics would not exist but for a lack of food and love.

A rather unhappy time began for Mary. For quite a while her certificate of excellence from the chef of the St. Denis was anything but a recommendation—as can well be imagined. This the maliciously smiling M. d'Albert had known perfectly well. For several months, therefore, she worked as a washerwoman or laundry maid in a hotel, making secret visits to the kitchen and sniffing the air like a cat.

Once she initiated an affair with the cook. The relationship did not last: the cook was a good lover, but his cooking was lousy, and that settled the matter for her.

She found jobs as an assistant in private households. She rarely stayed longer than a few weeks, mainly because she tended to quarrel with the cooks (usually women) by lifting the lid off the pot without asking permission, by criticizing their dishes or even accusing them of incompetence. No doubt she was usually right. Americans are quite inflexible in their eating habits, and were even more limited in Mary's time than today; if a cook could prepare a set of four or five dishes to the satisfaction of a family, she could count on a lifelong position. Occasionally, though, Mary would have a run-in with the lady of the house, who frequently had nothing better to do than to spy on her servants or tempt them to steal, be it only a dollar bill—an old trick: you "accidentally" dropped a dollar on the stairway and waited to see if the help kept it or returned it. A reliability test that Mary passed each time by handing over the bill with an ironic curtsy. Sometimes, though, a fit of temper (a kind of atavism, an emotional dependence on the weather, occasioned, say, by a sudden hailstorm) would betray her peasant origins, and she'd

91

hurry off to fetch a dozen nails and hammer the bill to the banister. Naturally, she'd be fired without notice for that. Aside from these occasional outbursts, though, she was well liked for her gaiety and good spirits; children were drawn to her because she was still close to them in age and manner, and the gentlemen appreciated her good looks.

The world turned.

In 1873 Bakunin published *State and Anarchy*, Nietzsche came to the end of his *Untimely Meditations*, Bruckner finished his Third Symphony in D Minor. In 1874 Winston Churchill was born and embarked on a long career of fundamental failure, which didn't change until late in life; Emile Zola wrote *The Belly of Paris*, a book that would no doubt have interested Mary, and England's industrial productivity was outstripped by that of its former colony, now called the U.S.A. In 1875 Bismarck expressed outrage at the French military buildup, and cynics scribbled slogans like "Socialism is the opium of the people" on the walls of university toilets; in New York, Helen Blavatsky founded the Theosophical Society. In 1876 Bizet's *Carmen* flopped in Paris; in England someone invented a bicycle with a recoil brake, and, for the first time ever, the presence of ladies at a sports tourney was noted (and noted with pleasure): it was during the first six-day bicycle race in Birmingham, and the ladies were laced up to the neck, to be sure, with imposingly stuffed derrières . . .

In 1876 Mary Mallon was on her way to her first job as a real cook. She had achieved this without an agency, without recommendations, thanks only to a somewhat grandiloquent notice in a newspaper.

24

Pierrepont Street, Brooklyn: the four-story residence of Louis Kotterer, Esq., his wife, Gwendolyn, née de Roche, and family. Mr. Kotterer was a hefty man in his mid-fifties without a single hair on his head; his wife was forty-seven and frail, which at the time was considered a very French quality for a lady to have. They had three children—a girl named Cathy and a set of twins named Raoul and Louis junior. Cathy had sexy hips, but her neck was much too long. And there was a maid, Angela, who was forty years old, came from Palermo, and let it be known by the sad songs she sang that she hadn't found a man to marry and had no children. She was very devoted to Mary, which Mary appreciated, though she found it incomprehensible.

She learned from Angela everything worth knowing about the family: for example, that Cathy slipped fresh rose petals into her underwear whenever she was to meet a lover, and that you could always tell the next morning whether they had exchanged anything more intimate than a kiss. If they hadn't, the petals would be lying on the rug of her room, and if no petals could be found there, you could logically conclude Cathy had left them lying somewhere else. Raoul Kotterer, the second-born twin, was studying engineering and had invented an apparatus to wake him up as soon as his penis began to erect. He was a body builder and spent hours lifting weights; he had crushed two toes of his left foot by dropping a particularly heavy pair of dumbbells on them, which gave him a slight limp. The firstborn twin, Louis junior, emotionally disturbed at being called "Junior" when in fact he'd been born eight minutes before Raoul and was therefore the elder son, wrote in a journal until the late hours of the night. He had originally wanted to become a naval officer but was afraid of water. He had never learned to swim, but you could see him on the docks in the company of young sailors. One evening he displayed an anchor tattoo on his upper arm, causing his mother such sorrow that she contracted shingles. She groaned for nights on end, and in her delirium spoke only French, which was very annoying, since no one in the family besides her had any command of this noble language. She was convalescing, slowly.

Louis Kotterer-de Roche, Esq., was the proprietor of a private bank the physical dimensions of which scarcely exceeded those of a drugstore. No one had ever been seen to open an account there, which is not as strange as it sounds, for Mr. Kotterer was a loan shark: short-term loans at 100 percent interest. Which is why on the top floor of his Flatbush Avenue bank he kept five burly card-playing Chinamen, who, when faced with a difficult case (of which there were many), understood *only* Chinese.

Such was the family history according to Angela, who carried the meals from the kitchen to the dining room. Mr. Kotterer introduced the new cook, but no one deigned to look at her, contenting themselves instead with bowing their heads and folding their hands in grace. That is the advantage of the pious: they can put their arrogance in God's invisible hands.

One evening, Mary decided to prepare an Italian meal. First she had Angela serve a salad, then roast rabbit and polenta. She prepared ice-cooled peaches for dessert. The family exchanged speechless looks, left knives and forks untouched. Within five minutes Angela had brought the plates back to the kitchen. Mr. Kotterer himself soon followed, to tell Mary, in a voice that was not at all unfriendly, that she was fired; his and his family's idea of a good meal was a T-bone steak. He drew a full week's salary from his wallet. Mary thanked him and asked Angela to serve the peaches. This seemed to meet with success, for Mary, who was listening in the kitchen, could hear the sound of clinking cutlery and a general smacking of lips.

Unfortunately.

Mary embraced the weeping Angela and left the house on Pierrepont Street.

When the *Times* published the joint obituary for Mrs. Gwendolyn Kotterer-de Roche and her son Louis junior, Mary had already found a new employer. She knew nothing of the event. Nor did she learn that Mr. Kotterer, having been stricken by fate more severely than some of his clients (or so he thought), decided from then on to charge no more than 75 percent interest on his loans. Thus life has its good side too.

25

Nowadays only wealthy homes in this city have open fireplaces. Firewood—you buy it in flower shops—is as expensive as sandalwood was a hundred years ago. But anyone looking for a cozy hearth can find it during the Christmas season by switching on his TV after the late late show: at least one channel uses the picture of a wonderfully blazing fireplace during station breaks and after the end of broadcasting—a totally safe, odorless fire that exudes no warmth whatsoever, a ghostly figment of the electronic age. How great, in comparison, was the childish pleasure Italian artists found in painting trompe l'oeil window shutters on a naked wall.

Well, if I had come up with the idea thirty years ago that one day people would cultivate trout in four-cornered fish ponds the size of a swimming pool, probably no one would have disputed it. Maybe we already had such things fifty years ago. But if I had predicted that grown men, amateur fly-fishers, dressed in the garb of the professional angler, their sou'-westers pulled down over their foreheads, equipped with all conceivable professional gear, would one day stand, not at the shore of a Canadian mountain lake, but by the edge of one of these artificial ponds, trout fishing, I think people would have laughed. And they would have laughed even harder if I claimed that these same men would pay admission fees of five dollars or more, and that as soon as they succeeded in hooking a trout they would carefully detach the hook and, in accordance with the rules of the establishment, put the fish back into its concrete pond.

My daughter, Lea, came to visit this weekend and was eager to read what I had written so far. She said she couldn't read in my presence, so she disappeared with the manuscript into her old room, which still looks the way it did when she was in high school—pennants on the walls, diplomas, and even one or two somewhat plucked-looking toy animals.

I have to admit I waited rather nervously. What would she think of it? Too grotesque? Lea has a sense of humor, so long as you don't ask her whether she's found Prince Charming yet.

I leafed without real interest through several pounds of the Sunday *Times*, something people of my circle pretend we can't do without. But what does that mean, "circle"? What a word! As a matter of fact, I don't even socialize with other doctors.

When Lea finally returned, she cleared her throat and put the manuscript on my desk.

"It's OK," she said. She remained cool. The up-and-coming M.D.

"And?" I asked.

Lea shrugged, let herself drop into an armchair, and pulled a pack of Marlboros out of her purse.

"I bet you think I have a preference for little girls." I think a father's more likely to feel embarrassed at being understood by his children than the other way round.

"Why shouldn't you?" she asked. "You did choose to become a pediatrician and not a gerontologist, right?"

"That's true," I said, yet I was surprised for a moment. "And what else? Is it all too grotesque?"

"Why too grotesque?"

"I mean the way people die. Do you think being a doctor has made me callous?"

"Of course you're callous, but no more callous than anyone who reads the newspaper."

I was a little annoyed, and started to defend myself with arguments she hadn't even provoked. Dying, I said, is always a tragic event while it's happening, even an individual's dying—*especially* an individual's. But given some distance in time, the whole thing flattens out, and what was once a reality gets twisted in time—"like the image in a funhouse mirror," I said.

Lea interrupted me, a little rudely.

"Who are you really trying to waste your time on?" she asked. "This is a story, not a medical report. When we were kids you told us hundreds of stories about Typhoid Mary and you always laughed, and so did we."

I was astonished.

"Maybe you should look up a gerontologist after all," she said, "your memory's definitely not in good shape. I remember you once told us a story about Mary serving a meal to a gathering of prospective heirs. They had a lawyer with them who was supposed to arbitrate some quarrel over the estate, there was even a brawl in the house. At any rate, the lawyer had to send everyone home and adjourn the meeting for weeks."

"And then?" I asked, amused.

"Well, everyone died of typhoid fever and the money went to some lazy bum of a nephew."

"Really?" I wanted to hear more of the stories I used to tell Lea.

The doorbell rang.

"Just keep on making up stories about how people died," Lea said. "But let them be rich people. Only Dickens could make anything out of poor people dying. Besides, only rich folks could afford a cook."

She stood up and kissed me on the forehead. "Sleep well, Dad, and don't commit any malpractice on yourself."

A couple with the names O'Brien and Appleton lived on the corner of Madison Avenue and Thirty-sixth Street, in Murray Hill. The walls were covered with dark green velvet, as was fashionable then, and wherever you looked you saw arrangements of huge plush sofas and armchairs in an irritating layout: each of the many seating accommodations stood back to back with its mate, as in a hotel lounge. Mr. O'Brien, real estate dealer and "honorary consul for the Argentine," and Mrs. Appleton, his widowed sister-in-law, lived together. O'Brien regularly donated enormous sums to the Lighthouse for the blind: years ago, at a charity ball, he had exchanged such vehement toasts with a friend that both glasses had shattered and a splinter had penetrated O'Brien's right eye and destroyed the pupil. The two friends broke off all contact after that.

As for Mrs. Appleton, she had been living in the almost perpetually half-dark apartment ever since the death of her husband, fifteen years before. She suffered from edema and had converted to Catholicism because she believed in a causal connection between the ulcerous sores on her feet and Christ's stigmata. Her favorite foods were cucumbers and bananas. She devoured an immense quantity of the latter, throwing the skins on the floor from whatever plush seat she happened to be on, always with a brusque finality, as if now she had definitely had enough.

It is perhaps understandable that this couple was constantly being abandoned by its hired help. They had endless quarrels, for Mr. O'Brien had slipped more than once on one of those banana peels and felt, perhaps not unreasonably, that he had cause to fear for the safety of his second eye.

It happened that Mary showed up for her first day of work at precisely the moment when Mr. O'Brien had once again lost his balance and fallen to the floor. Mary administered first aid in the form of a bandage on the forehead. Mrs. Appleton observed the scene over her shoulder through a lorgnette, shaking her head in disgust. Mr. O'Brien, still winded, said he didn't want to eat anything now, just to sleep, and told Mary in a few rough words where she could find her room.

When Mary got up at seven and went down to the parlor to clean up, she found a shopping list that insulted her culinary sensibilities. She was to buy six pounds of bananas, eggs, kosher pickles, and a loaf of Russian pumpernickel. And she was to replenish Mr. O'Brien's liquor cabinet. "Just booze," the note said—fortunately, for there wouldn't have been any way to determine his favorite brand from the dozen empty bottles that stood there. And for his dinner he wanted lamb chops and string beans. For hours Mary searched for a bakery that carried Russian pumpernickel, only to find it in the grocery around the corner. Since her new bosses had said they slept till noon, she took a walk home to the shack she shared with Chris.

At two o'clock, Mr. O'Brien and Mrs. Appleton were still asleep in their separate rooms. A glass and an opened bottle stood on a little table, from which Mary concluded that Mr. O'Brien had gotten up, taken a morning nip, and gone back to bed.

In the evening, Mary fried two lamb chops and cooked some beans, which Mr. O'Brien found much too tough. The next time Mary cooked the beans until they began to disintegrate. He seemed to like them that way, for he gave her a nod, whereupon Mrs. Appleton raised her lorgnette and focused a stare upon Mary. After dinner Mary had to bring Mr. O'Brien a copper basin full of water and sea salt for a footbath, then add more hot water every quarter hour.

Mrs. Appleton did not trust Mary with household money, and only after endlessly studying the receipts (chewing bananas all the while) would she repay Mary's expenses to the precise dollar and cent.

On the morning of her thirteenth day of work, Mary heard Mrs. Appleton groaning and moaning. Finally she entered her room without knocking. Mrs. Appleton complained of a headache. She was bleeding from the nose. Since the windows were closed, the stench of feces was immediately apparent. She brought Mrs. Appleton a glass of water and put a pot of tea on her bedside table. Then she energetically shook Mr. O'Brien out of his sleep; he had a hangover and was doubly disgruntled at being awakened so early. Not until Mary poured a glass of water in his face did he sit up, in a rage, throw a pillow at her, and roar at her to leave the house immediately. She was only too glad to do so. She removed twenty dollars from Mrs. Appleton's badly hidden privy-purse, packed her valise, and left.

Chris Cramer was surprised to see Mary back so soon with her valise, and asked what had happened. Mary didn't answer, and he lapsed into silence as well.

A few days later, Mary took a walk through Murray Hill to find the grocery that carried Russian pumpernickel. The store was closed "due to a death in the family." From neighbors she learned that the baker's wife had died the night before. Typhoid was suspected, perhaps an epidemic. Mary hurried away.

As soon as she got home she went to bed and chased her premonitions away like bad dreams. Chris Cramer read aloud from the newspaper: a typhoid epidemic had already spread through more than half of Murray Hill.

"What's typhoid?"

"A disease from bad water," he replied. "It's no wonder, the water's polluted all over the city. But rich people get their water direct from the mountains."

"That's nonsense," said Mary, a little arrogantly. "I've never seen rich people drink water direct from the mountains, and besides, some rich people have died of typhoid."

"Well, you may be right in a philosophical sense," Chris Cramer said, and immersed himself in a book which proved that only the wealthy benefited from technical progress.

Mary informed him she would no longer work as a cook. She would do piecework in a textile factory from now on.

*   *   *

The piecework put her into a state of half sleep, and she dreamed of having a child. Once her supervisor invited her into a saloon for a glass of beer, and Mary flirted with him. He was a tall dark-haired fellow, handsome, too, and one day she followed him into the warehouse where the bales of cloth were stored. She let him take her, with indifference at first, until she imagined the other women envying her, after which she began to enjoy herself. Every morning a half hour and every afternoon the same. A pleasant task for a male supervisor. When she missed her period, she lived in fear for several days. Much as she would have liked to have a child, she knew that would mean the end to her immaculate marriage to Chris Cramer. An unborn child wasn't worth the price. She quit her job, spent hours sitting in church, prayed to the Almighty, begging him to show some understanding for her special situation. After all, she argued, God himself had had all sorts of problems when his Son was born on Earth. She found mercy the very evening Chris Cramer asked her if she'd like him to arrange for a friend to father a child for her. Just as she gratefully embraced him, the cramps in her womb told her that there was no more cause for worry.

She remained careful, tried not to fall into temptation. For almost a full year she received a handsome salary for a once-a-week cleaning job—one of the German women at the market had gotten her the position—in a highly elegant and rather strange apartment belonging to a red-bearded eccentric named Robert Diffany. One morning the apartment was empty and workmen were tearing off the wallpaper.

Soon after that she took a job as an assistant cook with a Mrs. Perry Bolt, the widow of a divorce lawyer who had been shot by a client's wife. A month after

Mary started working, the chief cook died; a day after her funeral Mrs. Bolt passed away as well.

Mary found new positions: one with a Mr. and Mrs. Ralph Brettschneider, owners of a funeral parlor and a coffin workshop; they died. Another with a furrier named Thomas Bergen, who supposedly died of an infection from cutting his thumb while handling a poisoned fox. Mary had cooked. She helped out in a kitchen for a wedding party. The newspapers reported a new wave of typhoid. And now I intend to lose sight of her wanderings for several years.

27

By the turn of the century, "Typhoid Mary" had become a stock figure of popular horror stories—not just in New York, but in other northeastern cities, especially in Boston and Philadelphia. I'm fairly certain that my grandfather was right in suspecting that Mary actually lived in Philadelphia during the early eighties: "Good old Mary's in Philly now," it says in his calendar—with three question marks and an exclamation point added in the margin. Presumably she fled Philadelphia head over heels; I find in a local Philadelphia paper of the summer of 1882 an appeal by the editors to a certain Mary Martens, hired cook of the John Lafayette Otis-Berenson family, asking her to report as soon as possible to either the editors or the family itself, who wished to recompense her for her selfless devotion to their two children during the recent typhoid epidemic.

I presume it was either then or after a few other outbreaks of typhoid that she returned to New York. Much later, George A. Soper reports that Mary told him New York had always been her real home, because ever since her arrival there she had never felt comfortable anywhere else. Her brief stay in Philadelphia took place in the year Franklin Delano Roosevelt was born and Ralph Waldo Emerson died, the year Edison built the first electric plant in Mary's favorite city and Robert Koch, about whom we shall have more to say, discovered the tubercle bacillus.

That Mary had returned to New York by 1883 we know from an ad she put in the *Times*, a more modest one than her previous notices; that is, she no longer presented her culinary skills as her main asset, but stressed her ability as a caretaker for elderly couples and her experience in complying with special health regimens in her cooking.

The first response arrived the very next day, in the form of a letter signed only with initials. She was invited to present herself at Washington Square Park the next Wednesday at 11:00 A.M. She was to wear a yellow hatband, so that the coachman could recognize her. Financial terms could be discussed later. If she did not find the offer appealing, she need only respond by not showing up at the appointed place and time. Yours very truly.

Chris Cramer's remark Wednesday morning that it might be the invitation of a sex maniac did not intimidate her, and a half hour later she arrived at Washington Square with a bright yellow ribbon around her lacquered straw hat. The letter had not specified any particular corner or house for her to wait at. She walked nervously to and fro. As the bells struck eleven she heard hoofbeats behind her, and with a quiet "Whoa" a man's voice brought a two-horse coach to a halt at her side. The carriage was dark blue, and the coachman wore a hat like Napoleon Bonaparte's. The door opened, and a man's hand helped her climb in. The windows were covered on the inside with black paper; for several minutes all Mary could make out were the outlines of a man's face. When she finally dared look at him more closely, she saw that the lower half of his face was covered by a scarf. Was he just not saying anything or was he speaking so quietly that the rumbling, clattering wheels drowned out his voice? She waited, full of foreboding. Why, for God's sake, had she stepped into this carriage?

Eventually the sounds of the city subsided and she believed she could hear birds chirping. The wheels rolled more softly and with a springier motion, perhaps on a dirt road. She gave a start when finally the man next to her began to speak.

"I have been entrusted with an assignment by a very important person," he said. "This person, who will possibly pay you a visit in a few months, has asked me to inform you of everything you need to know, without prettifying the difficult task that awaits you. I think it would be best, therefore, if I explained the nature of the difficulty right away. Your duty will be to take care of a child, an abnormal child. A mongoloid. Do you understand?"

Mary whispered, "Yes."

"Your salary does not need to be discussed." Mary nodded. "Your job is not easy. You will watch the child, take walks with her, play with her; and prepare the few dishes children love—pancakes, rice pudding, applesauce, some chopped meat once in a while . . . well, you know about these things." Mary froze for a moment. "The child needs care. Maybe not for very long. Mongoloids rarely reach what's called a ripe old age." The voice sounded cold.

Silence. The silence was interrupted by a stifled curse from the coachman as a flock of sheep blocked the way. "Are you willing?" She nodded. "Excellent," the man said. "The house is very, very large, you will like it. Every day a man will drop by from Port Chester. He will buy whatever you need in the way of foodstuffs and so on in the village, and if you have any further wishes, he will convey them to me." After a pause he added: "Of course, we are well aware of your connection with the young man Chris Cramer. We know about his political activities as well, but that doesn't bother us. The person who sent me would not object to your receiving visits from him. However, we would have to ask that your friend maintain the strictest discretion, and you, my dear miss, can count on our discretion as well. We—that is, the person who sent me and I—have had you under observation for a long time. We are certainly not qualified to make a judgment as to the medical reasons." He paused again. "You are a destroyer."

Mary sobbed in horror and covered her face with both hands. "No, no, no," she cried, "none of that is true, it's just coincidence, lies and coincidence. I would never, never hurt anyone, never!"

The man put an arm consolingly around her shoulders. "Calm yourself, miss, it's not your fault, it's Nature playing some kind of trick, and that's what caught our interest. Please don't worry anymore, forget what I said. A stay in the country can't help but do you good. Calm down and relax. Everything will be just fine."

They did not talk after that. The coachman's voice lovingly called the horses to a halt.

"Step out, look around." The man's voice sounded imperious again. "Take your time. I'll wait."

When she stepped out she was nearly blinded by the reflection of light off the facade of a white house built in the neo-Grecian style of the American South. Two huge elms reached far above the house into the sky and cast their black shadows onto the roof. In the doorway stood a girl of about four, her smile radiant and full of unsuspecting candor, her arms stretched out toward Mary. Mary smiled and laughed back, walked up to her, knelt down, and folded her arms around the child, stroking and kissing her. She stood up and hurried back to the coach. The door opened immediately from inside, and the man's voice invited her in again.

"Yes," she said. "Yes, I will take care of the child. I will take really good care of her, please tell that to the person who sent you. What's the girl's name?"

"Caroline," he replied. "Just Caroline, is that clear?"

"Yes," Mary repeated, "yes, Caroline."

28

Mary felt no homesickness for New York, and no desire to return to work as a family cook. Caroline responded to her with spontaneous love, as is often the case with such children, and Mary's maternal instinct awoke with the swiftness and unrestraint of a passion. There was something in this overwhelming tenderness, too, that told her nothing could happen to the child. She prayed before going to sleep and informed God she would sin against His commandments and kill herself if any harm should come to this child.

She played with Caroline and let her play by herself, but always kept an eye on her. She took to gardening again, for the first time since she was a little girl. She worked long hours in the beautiful, wildly overgrown garden, planting flowers and vegetables of all kinds. The trustee in charge of shopping for Mary in Port Chester turned out to be a handsome, cheerful fellow who lived in the neighborhood, a farmer's son and himself the father of three children, whom he occasionally brought along to play with Caroline. He and Mary soon became good friends, but he refused to let a single word about his employers pass his lips. Once she took a trip to Manhattan with him and the children to buy some cloth and visit Chris Cramer; the next day, the young trustee delivered a letter to her in which she was politely requested to refrain from taking future trips of this sort with the child. Once again the brief note was signed only with initials.

Mary cooked. Caroline ate barley soup, small chunks of meat with chopped vegetables, rice pudding and applesauce. She talked and chattered, and her utterances, which sounded incomprehensible to others, were for Mary a language with clear and unmistakable meanings, a giving and receiving of impressions and thoughts. She was a mother.

Chris Cramer showed up every two weeks, either walking the long way from Manhattan or catching a ride with a farmer who was driving his vegetable cart home from the city markets. He always brought books or newspapers with him, and Mary watched him reading or playing with the child. She threw all his reading material into a shed and eventually burned it in a bonfire she made of the first autumn leaves and dry twigs. Only the works of Charles Dickens captured her imagination, and soon they became her favorite books.

She also read books by Horatio Alger, Jr., for Chris Cramer was still addicted to him despite the imminent world revolution, which presumably would obviate the need to help doddering millionaires across the street.

113

Whenever he came to visit, he would almost immediately withdraw to a darkened room and go to sleep on a couple of jute sacks. If it weren't for Mary, he would just as soon have spent all his hours in the twilight of a shed rather than exposing himself to sunlight and fresh air.

All this happened in 1884, the year the causes of tetanus, diphtheria, cholera, and typhoid fever were discovered by Nicolaier, Löffler, Gaffky, and Koch.

The century advanced toward its last decade, and Mary's four years of happiness with the child passed like the blinking of an eye. On special holidays, baskets with presents would arrive, and once a year Mary had to write a report on Caroline's physical condition. She added a great deal more than that about Caroline, convinced there must be a mother somewhere (perhaps she was sick) who would want to know everything about her child.

Mary was in her early thirties.

29

New York weathered its perpetual agony with an enormous will to live. There are pictures from the time that surpass by far what I saw in the way of garbage, rot, and filth during the 1968 garbage strike. Once citywide electrification began to illuminate the streets at night, there must have been a gorgeously lurid revelation of decay.

Fortune has nothing in common with a butterfly. It was a summer evening and Mary and Caroline were chasing after a butterfly that wouldn't let itself be caught and neither of them was really trying to catch. It was a funny game of falling down again and again, and it made them laugh. Then the sound of trotting hooves drew near, and Mary was afraid, as she had been the first time she saw the coachman with the Napoleonic hat. Once again, the windows were black. The horses stopped, pawed the ground. The coachman did not move, and Mary walked toward the coach as if hypnotized. The door opened a crack, just wide enough to reveal five fingers clad in black leather, one of which beckoned her. She stepped closer.

"Stop right there," said the voice, the same voice she had not been able to forget after all these years, months, and weeks. "You did the best you could." The man even laughed. "Nevertheless, you will be paid as handsomely as I promised."

Mary turned to look at Caroline. She was still running after the butterfly, screaming with joy. Mary was unable to conceal her fear and anger. "You want her now? This minute?"

"Calm down," said the man. "You still have a few days to take leave of her."

"Did I do something wrong?" Mary shouted.

"That's difficult to answer. You were good to her, we know that. But we expected something different from you. Stay where you are!"

Mary had stepped closer to the coach. "What did you expect from me? What?"

The man cleared his throat. "I'm not the one who decided this, you know that."

Mary screamed and wanted to step closer so she could see the man. Without even taking aim first, the coachman snapped his whip, and the end of it whistled past her face.

"Surely you know that we have identified you as Typhoid Mary," the man answered now. "We know you. One word from my superior and you will never find another job. Not even as a washerwoman. Do you understand now what it was we wanted from you? Consider our situation for a moment—whatever could become of a child like that?"

Mary turned to Caroline, who had stopped running and stood still, listening. Mary was quivering. "What kind of people are you?" she said. "What sort of people, damned God in heaven!"

"You will receive your just reward. And more so—believe me, Miss Mallon." Then an order to the coachman: "Move on." The coachman obeyed, the horses stepped into motion.

Mary ran after the coach. "Leave her with me! I'll always stay with her and never ask another question. Please! Please!"

She stumbled over a stone and fell to the ground. When she looked up, the coach had disappeared behind a thicket of trees. Caroline was crying. Mary hurried back and with seeming gaiety seized the girl (who had become large and heavy since Mary first saw her) and whirled her round and round. Caroline shrieked with pleasure.

When evening came she put the girl to sleep with a song and some comical rhymes, then went up to the attic and brought down two leather bags and stuffed them full of clothes, and wrapped up some food as well. She waited until midnight. She was convinced Caroline could manage a twelve-mile hike—at least. Then they'd take a train to the Canadian border. She hadn't woken the child yet. Then a suspicion prompted her to look out the window. Standing in the courtyard, his legs spread and his whip tucked under his arm, was the coachman with the Napoleonic hat.

She turned off the light. She knew there was nothing to be done, and finally, exhausted, she fell asleep.

Caroline's bed was empty the next morning. She was gone. On the kitchen table lay a sealed envelope with a check for a thousand dollars and a slip of paper with the words "Keep quiet."

A thousand dollars—a real fortune. But it would have been a double sin to give thanks to a God she despised.

Two days later she left the house.

30

The goal, according to someone whose name I forget, is to create a society that no longer needs heroes. Splendid—a simply delightful idea, since everyone tries so hard to keep from having to be a hero.

Our day-to-day opportunism allows for only one kind of hero: the man who pushes himself to the lead of all the other opportunists. Just look at them carrying on, the politicians, the public speakers of every stripe, the writers with their intellectual halos, the whole bumbling tribe of "just folks" chumming up to the poor-in-character. (I'm not speaking of the poor of the Sermon on the Mount, whose downhill ride seems to have no foreseeable end.)

It has become impossible to be a hero. A hero has to

be chosen by fate, there is no other way. It's not enough to like or even love the so-called common people. Mahatma Gandhi despised the masses. He once said that he felt much safer on his path when the masses spat on him, and that uncritical reverence bored him to distraction.

Unfortunately, no hero's role ever offered itself to me—at least none I would have recognized as such; whereas I very often accepted the role of courageous doctor who knows the difficulties and risks of his profession, and traded in my own sense of right and wrong. If I hadn't, what doctor worth his salt would have protected me in a malpractice suit, which could have happened anytime? Sinclair Lewis refused to accept the Pulitzer prize for *Arrowsmith* because he felt the central character (described as selfless and heroic) was not typical of the American medical community. And who among my colleagues wants to remember the scandalous treatment of Semmelweis by his colleagues, among them a certain Professor Virchow in Berlin, a great celebrity in his day?

I'm getting lost in details, I know. But when I look out my eleventh-floor window at night, all I see is thousands of brightly lit windows, details everywhere, behind which people live, hate, work.

Since in the little time I have left I'm unlikely to discover a hero, I hereby proclaim Mary Mallon, alias Maria Caduff, a hero. She had no choice. That's why.

> Leave a mark. Write the names
> that torment you on a toilet wall.
> Draw a line. Write: Whoever can piss
> this high, report to the fire department.
> Leave a mark: a child or a brainchild.
> Someone knows you're coming back.
> Irrigate your neighbor's desert.

Maybe he planted seed there
and no longer knows it. The one next door.
And don't plant ivy. It grows by itself.
Don't commit a crime. It'll frighten you
when coming back, you don't know the reasons
    why.
Leave a mark. Steal from the rich.
Despise poverty. It will recognize you.
Spit on money. It will welcome you.
Have your portrait painted. Build houses. Invent
    a lie
that makes everyone say: He started it!
And people will fear this knowledge.
Leave a mark. A message. A word.
Invent a cross between bird and flower.
Give a day's wages to the first child
that crosses your path, and smile at her.
Leave a mark. So that a hundred eleven years
    from now,
you'll rediscover the world as your home.

I wrote this poem for Mary in the name of Chris Cramer.

31

Mary regarded self-pity as an emotional disease for which one has only oneself to blame. She missed the child, and she also missed the colors of the autumn countryside, the wine-red, blood-red, and yellow glow of the leaves as the copper-red sun sank to the horizon a little sooner each day. But that was all. She discovered a few of the most elegant shops on her walks between the St. Nicholas Hotel and Thirty-fourth Street, where she bought two expensive dresses and was escorted out the door by graciously bowing salesgirls who were as elegantly dressed as their customers. "To what address may we have the dresses delivered, madam?" they asked with discreet curiosity. She identified herself as Miss Marlow from Boston, resident at the Hotel St. Denis.

She had found out that a certain M. Jules d'Albert had molted his worn chef's feathers and emerged a full-fledged hotel owner, having ingested the entire establishment by first impregnating and then marrying the previous owner's daughter. The next day Mary drove up to the hotel in a carriage and was ushered in, and a bellboy hurried off to fetch M. d'Albert. To her surprise, he actually came into the lounge, carrying in his hands the silver-and-violet cardboard box that contained her new clothes. He had grown chubby, with a bald head and a greased, pointed mustache. He declared himself thrilled to see Miss, ahem, Marlow—after all these years. Dancing and tripping with politeness, he escorted her to his office, where Mary gently and unhesitatingly informed him that she wished to have a new letter of recommendation crediting her Mary Marlow—with having been the St. Denis Restaurant's commercial traveler and specifying that she had left the establishment of her own choice.

M. d'Albert did not hesitate for a moment; the mere memory of the epidemic could have become at the very least unpleasant, even in this forgetful city, and so his ink-black pen sped vigorously across the page and signed it with a flourish. He then folded the sheet and put it in a padded envelope bearing the letterhead "St. Denis Hotel, Management." Then he bowed, glad to have gotten rid of her so quickly, and escorted her to the front door.

Chris Cramer's shack had hardly changed, except for the addition of a small wooden shed he had built and painted red. It was a veritable arsenal of tools, wires, spools, and rusty metal objects of indeterminable function, and here too, scattered among the debris, were large numbers of books and subversive pamphlets. He no longer spoke of the world revolution as if it were something you could pick up at a train station, unwrap, and let loose. He seemed sad, as if he had had to postpone his ideals. "Someday we're going to explode a bomb at Union Square and the rich'll finally wake up." Mary inquired quietly whether it wasn't the working class that needed to wake up. "The proletariat isn't mature enough yet," he replied, "we have to rid them of fear first." Mary nodded. She unpacked her new dresses and hung them over the clothesline in front of the door.

Little had changed on the street. Maybe its poverty had become more picturesque: ragged wash hung out to dry amid Neapolitan and kosher cooking smells; children shouting; the Polish fortuneteller next door whipping her lover's daughter with a rope hardened in glue; and from a basement apartment you could hear screams of pleasure from a woman who at this time of day was usually on a street corner being blessed with coins for being deaf, mute, and blind.

As ever, Chris Cramer kept his underwear on when he lay down on the mattress with Mary, and held her in his arms till she fell asleep. At least that's what he'd hoped. Mary stayed awake, for a long time.

32

Mrs. Stricker's employment agency dealt mainly in domestics: butlers, chambermaids, coachmen, gardeners, and private cooks. Her secretary had handed her the St. Denis's recommendation, and Mrs. Stricker came out of her office in person to scrutinize this Mary Marlow from head to toe, all the while playing with three intertwining rows of pearls slung around her neck; she always did this when she wanted to divert a distinguished client's attention away from her ugly pointed face. She invited Mary into her office—actually more a fashionable lounge full of lamps, plush, and brass statuettes.

"Mademoiselle," she began, "mademoiselle, I do not, for the moment, see a position that would be vacant for a lady of your special qualifications. Needless to say, I shall be able to find you a suitable position in due course, and I have absolutely no reason to question a recommendation from M. d'Albert—who is a personal friend of mine, incidentally. However, please understand that the ladies and gentlemen I cater to, especially the ladies, will, I believe, find you too attractive and— please consider this a compliment—too much of a lady— for gentlemen."

"I am a cook," Mary retorted stubbornly.

"There are dozens of excellent lady cooks in this city," came the answer, "who don't waste their talents on sauces and vegetable odors."

Mary stood up and left the room, trailed by Mrs. Stricker, who was whispering, and not just out of politeness, about certain other well-paid positions. Mary slammed the door shut behind her.

Yes, Mary had become a beauty. But how to capture female beauty in words, in this age of total visuality? It wasn't just the pale gray of her eyes that made her face so striking, but their luster and liveliness: feminine vitality. She had an attractive way of walking, too, each graceful step leading from the middle of her body; her skin radiated the freshness of country air, her hair reflected light, there was elegance in all her movements.

It was an altogether wonderful morning into which she stepped from the unpleasant premises of Mrs. Stricker's agency, the kind of morning that seems to have just been invented by the Creator. Mary stopped several times in front of shopwindows and mirrors until she found herself at the door of Mrs. Seeley's employment agency, almost as if she had been led there in her sleep.

Mrs. Seeley stood up behind her desk, a woman in her mid-thirties, as beautiful and noble-looking as the rich ladies in Horatio Alger's novels. It was the way Mary would have liked to look. "What can I do for you?" Mrs. Seeley asked in a friendly manner.

Mary searched in her pocketbook for the letter of recommendation, but couldn't find it. "I am a cook," she said, "I really am, but I have to go back and fetch my letter of recommendation. I'm sorry, I forgot it."

Mrs. Seeley interrupted her. She said she didn't doubt the existence of Mary's certificate. "And what sort of cooking are you especially versed in: French? Italian? Or general?"

The number of restaurants in New York City at the time is estimated at more than five thousand, but how many female cooks were wanted? "Do you really wish to work in a hotel restaurant again? Why don't you sit down?" Mary sat down, holding herself very upright, and dried her forehead with a silk handkerchief, while Mrs. Seeley pulled a large address book out of her desk and began to leaf through it. "No," Mary said, "I think I'd prefer a private household." Mrs. Seeley picked up her pen and asked for Mary's name.

"Mary, Mary Mallon," she said. "I don't have an address of my own at the moment, I'm living with relatives."

"Come back in three days, Miss Mallon, I'm sure we'll find something. Are you by any chance of German origin, Miss Mallon?"

127

Mary shook her head. "I'm Irish."

"I see," said Mrs. Seeley, "I thought I detected a slight German accent. But you wouldn't mind working for a German household, would you?"

"I wouldn't mind," Mary said. The interview was over. When she was out on the street she looked for the letter of recommendation again and found it was still in her pocketbook after all. She felt happy, and bought Chris Cramer a red scarf and a coat the shade of bottle green.

But fortune has nothing in common with red scarves and bottle-green coats. An evening walk to the Bowery would have reduced her to a state of livid terror. Among fruit stalls, candy stores, large and small theaters, and countless bars and restaurants catering to all the world's nations, there were also a great many "museums," as they called themselves, where for a few cents you could watch dressed-up dancing monkeys, three-hundred-pound women, a man with four ears, trained rats, and dwarfs with magician's hats; also lamplit pictures of earthquakes, burning theaters, sinking ships, and fire-spewing mountains. Not to forget the gallery of notorious women: poisoners and child murderers and necrophiliacs, and among them the image of a grim-looking cook with gnashing teeth and saliva dripping from her mouth into a steaming, poison-green caldron: "TYPHOID MARY."

33

It was November first when Mary arrived for her first day of work at the address Mrs. Seeley had given her, on Madison Avenue and Fortieth Street. She carried only a small valise with a few pieces of clothing, and when she saw St. Bartholomew's Church she stepped in, genuflected haphazardly, and went back outside without praying.

Mr. Carl Leichtner, who was scarcely older than Mary, was just about to leave his house. A maid stood next to a pail of water on the soapy sandstone steps, waiting for Mr. Leichtner to finish taking leave of his wife and walk down the stairs. Once he'd done so she slapped the pailful of water onto the steps and disappeared inside the house. Mr. Leichtner (who, incidentally, reminds me of the movie actor James Stewart, tall, with a nasal but pleasant voice), called out to her as she approached: "You must be Miss Mallon." They shook hands. "That's Mrs. Leichtner up there," he said, then scrutinized Mary's little valise and joked: "Is that all your luggage, or just the herbs and spices?"

The shouts of children could be heard inside the house; something wooden was tumbling downstairs. Without turning around, Mrs. Leichtner shouted, into space, as it were, and in German: "Will you cut out that darned noise!" She had cheerful and, for a New Yorker, unusually relaxed features. With a slight, casual movement of the hand she waved her husband good-bye once again. Didn't Mary look like his cousin, the one he had been in love with when he was sixteen, he shouted up to Mrs. Leichtner, who turned to Mary and greeted her.

They had arrived from Germany just three months ago, she said. Her husband was a representative of a German insurance company, and she hoped Mary wouldn't have too much trouble with her three children. They were nine, seven, and five years old, two girls and a boy, and she shouldn't hesitate to settle any disagreements with a little slap. The children hadn't found any friends yet, mainly because of the language problem.

While she explained all this with great kindness, Mary stood still, breathing deeply, completely motionless. She had heard little more than broken scraps of German at the markets since she had arrived in the country; now suddenly she was once again the little *Schwabengängerin*, standing at the front door of a German family on her first day of work.

"My God, is it your heart?" Mary heard a concerned voice. "Come in, I'll fetch a glass of water and some

valerian. My goodness, where did we put the valerian?"
The young woman hurried up the stairs.

The children stood in the door and gazed down at
Mary, their eyes large with curiosity.

Mary turned around, invaded by a sudden dread, and
ran as if for her life. Three blocks farther she crossed
the avenue, and continued running breathlessly until
she reached the church. Her steps echoed loudly. She
sat down in one of the pews and waited until her heart
had stopped racing. She couldn't cry. A block of stone
lay on top of her soul, or something more horrible,
some kind of vermin, and she prayed: Who am I? Why
are you doing this to me? Is what I'm doing to others
part of you? I hoped you had forsaken me. Why didn't
you? I am a person. Why don't you just forget about
me? Why do you stick your nose in things that are none
of your business?

She fell silent. It was cold and dark in the church.
She shivered. When she rose to her feet, she felt hun-
gry and thirsty. She thought of peaches, lovely tender-
skinned peaches, and of the delicious treats she could
make with them.

131

34

She hid away in Chris Cramer's shack, dragged her mattress into another corner, wrapped herself in blankets and cushioned her head on the musty pillows. Half asleep, she heard men's voices. She slept and slept. She woke up after two days, filled every pot in the house with water and brought each of them to boil. Then she filled the zinc tub, bathed, got dressed, and cooked a bean-and-barley soup for eight men whom she didn't know and who addressed each other by number instead of by name. She opened the small valise and took out the sheet of paper with the two addresses Mrs. Seeley had written down for her. The second was that of Mr. John Spornberg. This address she liked, not only because Mr. Spornberg was, apparently, a bachelor, but because he lived in the residence hotel above Delmonico's, the famous restaurant at the corner of Fifth Avenue and Twenty-sixth Street.

In front of the feudal restaurant stood a black-skinned doorman with kid gloves and a gold-edged captain's hat. He raised a hand in a casual salute and asked if he could help her. Mary showed him her piece of paper, and he led her to the elevator. Mr. Spornberg was usually an early riser, the doorman said, but he had not left the house. "Are you the new cook?" he asked curiously, and grinned. "I wish you the best of luck, young lady," he said, then added, confidentially, tapping his forehead with his finger: "He's nice, Mr. Spornberg is, but a little bit ticktock. You'll see what I mean. Fifth floor."

Mr. Spornberg was already waiting by the elevator on the fifth floor, staring at his pocket watch. "This elevator is extremely irregular," he remarked. "Even when there are no stops, the fifth floor run shows a differential of up to eleven seconds. Damn, damn! I'll see the management hears about this!" Mr. Spornberg wore Persian slippers, just like Sherlock Holmes.

Mary brought out Mrs. Seeley's referral, and he seemed delighted. "But, but . . . Miss . . . um . . ."

"Miss Mallon," she answered.

"Please come in, Miss Mallon, it's just twenty steps to the door." With these words the portly gentleman waddled ahead, squat as a Japanese wrestler.

With each of his ponderous steps there grew a sound that resembled the ticking of clocks. Her ears had not deceived her: clock upon clock hung in the hallway of the apartment, and the living room too was a pandemonium of clocks. The floor was covered with a triple layer of rugs, but neither this nor the heavy velvet curtains drawn in front of the windows nor the camel's-hair blankets protecting the walls behind the clocks did much to muffle the sound. Mary felt slightly dizzy. She did not open her eyes again until she heard Mr. Spornberg's loud, deep voice. He wasn't speaking so much as shouting, and not at her but with a friendly smile at all the grandfather clocks that stood about him. Besides them, there was a clock seven feet around, which had been originally built for a train station, not to mention the cuckoo clocks of all sizes that surrounded it. And always the constant, incessant, hundredfold ticktock, ticktock, ticktock, with perhaps a fraction of a second's silence between a tick and a tock.

The question he had screamed into this racket was "What can you cook?" and since she didn't answer, he continued: "Everything? My favorite food is ham with peppercorns in applesauce! What? What else? Rice pudding with cinnamon for breakfast with some jasmine tea, nothing else! Can't stand fish! Too watery by nature! I need real nourishment, something substantial! Corn on the cob with butter! Roast pork and macaroni! Pig's knuckles in tomato with wild rice and a pot of coffee! Things like that! No salad!"

Mary began to take notes, or rather pretended to take notes, because the ticking made her hands tremble too much to write. "I'd like to see the kitchen!" she shouted.

Mr. Spornberg nodded and led her through a second room full of clocks hammering out the passage of time. She gave a sigh of relief. There were no clock sounds in the kitchen; nothing but hourglasses everywhere. She immediately shut the door, and Mr. Spornberg shouted a little more quietly. She would get used to the sounds, he said. He began to tell the story of his life. His father had been a mathematician, his mother had died in childbirth, his birth. His father had always needed total peace and quiet to concentrate on his work, and so the baby was always being put to sleep. By whom? Why, by the nursemaid, who else; and later the governess. He was always lying in the dark, and most of the time he slept. Probably he was given mild tranquilizers. When he got a little older, he couldn't tell sunrise from sunset. In fact, he had no sense of time at all until his father died.

"Would you be satisfied with twelve dollars a week!" he shouted. "Anything else you need you can always steal! Like all the help nowadays! Yes, yes, I'm glad you have your own place! I don't like having people around in the evening, I want my peace and quiet!" Mary signaled her agreement with his terms, adding, however, that she'd like a week's tryout before committing herself. Mr. Spornberg shrugged. Probably no cook ever lasts here more than a week, Mary thought, and asked for five dollars to buy her first groceries. Reluctantly he drew the bills from his wallet.

"Please bring me a pot of tea with cookies at five!"

She nodded and waved good-bye. Outside, trying to shake the ticking out of her head, she noticed that she remained deaf for several minutes. Her first intention was to go shopping for him just once, then disappear forever. But she didn't want to disappoint Mrs. Seeley, who had been so kind and tried so hard to find Mary a job. She decided to stay at least two or three weeks. Since she would be spending most of her time in the kitchen or shopping and would have to put up with the din of the living room only while setting the table and serving meals, the work would not be unbearable. And as it turned out, Mr. Spornberg was basically an amiable man, and his stinginess was pretended.

35

In the ticktocking course of the eighties, history was set both forward and back, as usual. The Italians were not just singing, they made a little excursion into Africa to subjugate and occupy Eritrea and Somaliland; in Russia, Czar Alexander II was murdered, and his successor founded the secret police group called the Okhrana; in happy Switzerland Johanna Spyri wrote *Heidi*, the story of a child; Arnold Böcklin painted the *Island of the Dead* and became famous. The first electric streetcar tinkled its way through Berlin; in the Egyptian "Valley of the Kings" Emil Bugsch-Bey found the mummies of forty kings. Now there's a decade for you!

On the eleventh day of her job, Mary found Mr. Spornberg weakened and sick on a couch in his living room. It was five o'clock, so she brought him a pot of tea and cookies. When she returned in an hour, the cup was untouched, and a fevery sweat was dripping from his brow.

She woke him up. "Mr. Spornberg," she said, "you are sick."

"Absolutely correct!" Mr. Spornberg yelled back. "I feel damned uncomfortable!"

"Should I call your relatives?"

"To hell with relatives!" he replied, with a voice that could no longer compete with the mighty ticktock of his clocks, and when Mary urged him to at least go to bed, he began to swear. Mary leaned down to him. Maybe, he said, maybe it *would* be better to call the doctor. Then he cursed again, and she realized he was railing at the entire medical profession, the "blood-suckers," as he called us.

Mary felt inexplicably threatened at the mere mention of the word "doctor." Mr. Spornberg pointed at the telephone, one of those new inventions she disliked even under ordinary circumstances. She finally obeyed— that is, she dialed the number. But when the receiver was picked up at the other end, she didn't say a word.

"Hello," said the voice, "who's there?" Finally she heard a laugh. "Why, it's you, Mr. Spornberg. Ticktock, ticktock!"

Mary still did not answer, and now the voice sounded concerned: "Mr. Spornberg! Hello! Mr. Spornberg!"

Mary hung up. She was in a panic. What on earth should she do? She ran downstairs and stopped there. Wasn't it cowardly of her to flee? No, she told herself. She hurried on, stopped again. She decided to go back. If the doctor came she would find some excuse to leave the house for a while. She ran up the stairs and down the hallway and heard a frightful noise. Not the tick-

137

tock of clocks, no—a crashing and crunching, as of heavy furniture. She opened the door.

Mr. Spornberg stood, with his back to the door, swaying precariously as he ripped the clocks off the walls with rigid fingers and let them tumble to the ground. The larger clocks already lay shattered on the floor. A tall, narrow grandfather clock lay on its back, the pendulum jutting out from its coffinlike casing like a stiff tongue. A push and a tug, and another clock toppled off its pedestal, clattering. "Help me, Mary, help me, please," he wailed. "I can't bear to hear it anymore. I can't stand it. Please, please!"

It was more than pity, it was rage that overcame Mary, the rage of a woman who could never hope for real happiness or peace. She began to fly about the room like a fury. She ripped the massive pendulum out of the toppled grandfather clock and swung it into the ticktocking time machines, stomping to pieces the wooden casings, hammering metal against metal. She hurled sheets of glass against the wall; wood splintered, cuckoo clocks burst open, clock springs uncoiled with a twang, clock hands flew like arrows about the room.

Mr. Spornberg stood in the middle of the room, smiling happily like a child, attempting to applaud with his feeble hands. Then his last strength left him, and he collapsed. Mary continued on her rampage until she noticed that he had fallen to the floor. At the same moment someone grabbed her by the wrist and ordered her to stop. Stop!

It was the doctor. Mr. Spornberg, dying, welcomed his family physician with a friendly smile. "Nice of you to come by, Dr. Rageet! How meaningless it was, all that time." He gestured toward the clocks. "And now this wonderful quiet! How wonderful!"

139

36

Perhaps the reader remembers that my grandfather's involvement with Mary Mallon—a sort of hobby in the beginning—was inspired by his friend and professional colleague George A. Soper, and that he eventually began to make his own separate and secret observations. Of course, he was well aware of the research and discoveries of Robert Koch, the German bacteriologist, who won the Nobel Prize for medicine in 1905. Whether Koch, the discoverer of the chronic-typhoid-carrier syndrome, ever heard of the case of Typhoid Mary, I have no idea. But I doubt it. George A. Soper's decision to postpone publication of his brief report until 1939 was, I am sure, an act of consideration for Mary.

My grandfather registered the case of his private

patient, John Spornberg, in his agenda but made no mention of the clock-smashing cook until later in life. Presumably he had not suspected any causal connection between Spornberg's death and Typhoid Mary. However, he does seem to have consulted Mrs. Seeley's agency, and Mrs. Seeley, who was still a beautiful woman, was able to recall a number of vivid details.

Shortly after Mr. Spornberg's death, Mary returned to Mrs. Seeley's office with a request for a new position. Her employer—so she said—had died of a heart attack. Julia Seeley offered Mary four prospective jobs. Three Mary rejected; Mrs. Seeley suspected it was because they were far from downtown and would keep her too far away from some secret lover.

Only once did she accept a job in the Bronx, and this was for one week in September. The Bronx had not yet become a borough of New York City, and it was a long way there and back. The house where Mary worked belonged to two aged sisters and their even older brother. According to Mrs. Seeley, no cook had ever been able to stand it long, for the two sisters harassed  their employees with compulsive mistrust and stinginess. Shortly after Mary had quit, or, more likely, fled, the two

141

sisters died. Strangely enough, sometime later a cheerful old man showed up at Mrs. Seeley's agency—it was the brother—and left an envelope with a good deal of money for "the most charming—and helpful—Miss Mallon."

Mary was frightened once again. A minor typhoid epidemic broke out in that area of the Bronx. Fifty-three people fell ill, four died. Ah, but wouldn't it be more important to report that an economic crisis erupted in the United States that would last until 1896? Or that a certain M. Dubois claimed to have found the remains of an ape-man in Java?

I'm finding it more and more difficult not to think of Mary Mallon as my own daughter. Am I using her as an instrument of revenge? For I too am that foolish old brother of two nagging sisters, who feigns ignorance of Mary's ability to bring about a truly equalizing justice. The justice every mortal, atheist or not, occasionally dreams of . . . Am I right?

Of course, my real daughter is Lea, a gifted, intelligent woman with a sense of humor, who stands on the threshold of a brilliant professional career and could not care less about concepts like "equalizing justice." Something to do with doctor's ethics, so called. I once knew a prostitute who surprised me with this confession: that she really liked men. But that was more than thirty years ago.

Something just occurred to me: I haven't once mentioned my father. There must be reasons why he never appears in my dreams. An excellent and much loved doctor, by the way. He, too, had a passion for ethics, going so far as to testify against his older brother in court—a first-rate dentist so talented he performed abortions on the side, which at the time cost little more than a filling.

Every family history is an abyss.

37

I first saw Mary Mallon thirty-two years ago," writes George A. Soper in his article. "She was five feet, six inches tall, a blond with clear blue eyes, a healthy skin color, and a somewhat determined mouth and jaw." My grandfather remembered her as slender and lithe, though Soper described her as somewhat more heavily built; but that may be because my grandfather met Mary (through Mr. Spornberg) several years before his colleague set eyes on her. One thing Soper, a friendly but timid man, did not fail to notice was that look of absolute determination. Perhaps Soper, a master over life and death in his own right, was not entirely insensitive to the special condition of an uncooperative patient; most doctors regard resistance to treatment as evidence of suicidal tendencies, and though

144

we don't like to admit it, such patients tend to quickly lose our sympathy.

"My discovery of Typhoid Mary was the outcome of an investigation made in the winter of 1906–'07 into an outbreak of typhoid fever in the house of Mrs. George Thompson, at Oyster Bay, N.Y. The place had been rented to a New York banker, General William Henry Warren, who had occupied it with his family of three and seven servants for the summer months. Late in August, an explosion of typhoid had occurred in which six of the eleven persons in the household were taken sick."

Since William Henry Warren was a prominent personality, an inquest was immediately initiated. Mrs. Thompson, the landlady, was less concerned for the life of the general and banker than about the remaining summer's rent she was losing. That summer, no fewer than 3,467 cases of typhoid were reported in New York City; roughly 700 of these resulted in death.

As an undergraduate medical student, Soper had happened to spend his Christmas vacation in Warrensburg, New York, in a house where typhoid kept breaking out at regular intervals, as if the place were nothing but the stage set for a play about some ancient curse. Soper had pulled the curtain on the drama: he had had the tenants put into quarantine and—with the owner's consent—had set the accursed house on fire. Not a plank, brick, or rafter was left unpurified, and the episode had earned him fame as an unflinching fighter in the war against epidemics.

"When I went to Oyster Bay," Soper continues, "the first thing I did was to get together all the essential facts about the outbreak: the dates of the attack, the diagnoses, and like information." At first Soper had trouble getting to the root of the matter. He neglected nothing, checked every detail; the research team that had done the groundwork, all colleagues of his, had performed a fault-less job, searching the house from the roof to the cellar, from the cistern to the lawn. Not a crack had been overlooked, not a single sanitary installation, from the pipes down to the cesspool.

Then something occurred to him. Soper was not unac-quainted with the phenomenon of the disease carrier. He had come across cases where a patient's urine re-mained infectious even a considerable time after the patient's restoration to health. Soper no longer hesitated. He gave instructions to the hospitals not to release patients before examining their urine. "It was hard to identify typhoid in the feces," he noted, "by current bacteriological methods." But Soper outgrew his own bacteriological infancy with a single daring move: he returned to the unfortunate summer residence of Gen-eral William Henry Warren, Esq., and began a point-by-point, or rather person-by-person, interrogation.

And there she was: the cook. The cook, he learned, had vanished long ago, but where had she gone? The moment the sickness had broken out, she had asked for her wages and left that very day. Mrs. Warren had given her only part of the unfinished week's pay. Mary had been a good cook, she said; a very good cook, but not really outstanding.

Here George Soper interrupted Mrs. Warren. Who had recommended this cook? Mrs. Stricker's agency, on Twenty-eighth Street.

Mrs. Stricker? The revolting lady who wanted to rent Mary out to rich men?

Indeed. Mrs. Stricker, however, insisted that she had never seen this Mallon woman. A middle-aged man had come to register name and credentials, and it was he, not Miss Mallon, who paid the usual commission in exchange for the family's address.

Soper knew only the name, nothing more. But what if it wasn't her real name? My grandfather, Irving Rageet, discovered in the "help wanted" ads in the *Boston Globe* (at that time the most widely read newspaper in the country) the notices of a cook "experienced in European and American cuisine," and always specifying "the New York area." Each and every notice was worded the same way, except that each time there was a different name: Elizabeth Brown, Jane Gardener, Denise Delpire.

38

I gather from my grand-
father's notes that it was he who was able to give Soper
a first approximate description of Mary, and as it turned
out later, this description basically matched that of Mr.
Spornberg's young cook. At the time, Mary was moving
from one job to the next with almost hectic haste:
sometimes she would leave her place of work after just
a few days. "I uncovered a series of seven household
epidemics," reports Soper. "My earliest record places
Mary Mallon at Mamaroneck. The date was September
4, 1900." The next year, 1901, Mary turned up in New
York City.

The new century had dawned. Leon Trotsky fled his
Siberian captivity for London; Emile Zola died; in Germany Aby Warburg founded the Library of the History

of European Culture, ninety thousand volumes and a picture archive (all of which had to be transported to London four decades later to save the collection from the Nazis); Valdemar Poulsen invented the high-frequency arc transmitter; R. F. Scott, exploring the Antarctic, discovered snow and ice and claimed them for Great Britain. Rudolf Virchow ended his mortal career after so thoroughly ruining that of his colleague Semmelweis. The Lindauer brothers replaced women's corsets with their new invention, the brassiere.

I wrote these lines last night, copied and edited them. When the pain gets too intense, I do what I've often done—leaf through the reference books on world history and contemplate all the things I've missed. Not to mention all the things I will miss, thank God—but let's get on with the story. What did Soper discover about Mary in New York City? A laundress had contracted typhoid and been taken to Roosevelt Hospital; the doctor, one Dr. Carlisle, failed to investigate further; servants are not that important. It seems that a few months later, Mary showed up in Dark Harbor, Maine, at the summer residence of Coleman Drayton, a New York lawyer. (This was the third time Mary left New York State.) Within three weeks seven people had taken sick in the household. No deaths. According to Mr. Drayton, who was not infected, Mary Mallon helped until everyone had recovered; someone had to stay up for nights on end, and it was Mary who volunteered. She didn't take a moment's rest for herself. When she left (explaining that a relative in Manhattan had fallen ill and needed her help), the lawyer gave her double her monthly wage, shook her hand, and immediately washed his hands, something most wealthy people used to do on the first of January after wishing their servants a happy New Year. Mr. Drayton's snobbery may have saved his life.

In 1904, Soper learned, there had been a report on a typhoid epidemic in the Henry Gilsey family of Sands Point, Long Island. Eleven people this time, four Gilseys and seven employees. A perfect equation, in terms of social arithmetic. For consider the opposite ratio: how could four servants provide a family of seven with anything like perfect service?

After the Oyster Bay episode, Soper hunted and waited. There must have been times when my grandfather thoroughly annoyed him by discovering new epidemics in New York precisely at the moment Dr. Soper was investigating outside the city. The two often played chess together. During these matches my perfidious forebear, who by day plied his trade with good-natured aplomb, assisting at childbirth or shutting dead eyes, liked to underscore an ingenious move of his knight or bishop with some remark having to do with Typhoid Mary, whereupon Soper would promptly lose.

Soper did not catch wind of Mary again until 1907, in Hackensack: an upper-class family, still healthy; two deaths in the domestic staff.

39

Shortly thereafter, Soper heard of a typhoid case in a building on the corner of Sixtieth Street and Park Avenue. The family's washerwoman had fallen ill, as had a young child. Soper went to the building, entered the apartment through a side entrance, and walked into the kitchen, where Mary was washing dishes. What happened there might have been a scene out of a Mack Sennett comedy. Soper—to his credit!—did not spare himself in depicting his failure.

With the instinct of a hounded creature, Mary seized the kitchen table with both hands and set it like a barricade between Soper and herself, waiting, watching. "Miss Mallon," said Soper, "I am not a policeman, I am a doctor, and I would like to ask you to listen to what I have to say." Mary remained motionless, like a cat.

Later Soper had this to say: "I suppose it was an unusual kind of interview, particularly when the place is taken into consideration. I was as diplomatic as possible." My grandfather seems to have had his doubts (which I share) as to whether such delicate diplomacy was feasible under the circumstances. For years she had eluded Soper's search like a phantom; by now the whole city, the whole country was cracking jokes about Typhoid Mary, and only Soper and my grandfather knew who she really was. "I had to say I suspected her of making people sick," he writes, "and that I wanted specimens of her urine, feces, and blood."

That single sentence sufficed. Mary yanked out the drawer of the kitchen table, grabbed a carving fork, shoved, or rather threw, the kitchen table aside, and approached Soper silently, with slow steps and lowered head.

"I passed rapidly down the long narrow hall, through the tall iron gate, out through the area, and so to the sidewalk. I felt rather lucky to escape." Almost naively he adds: "Apparently Mary did not understand that I wanted to help her."

Soper did not record his emotional condition immediately after this frightening encounter, but we can surmise that he was upset. To think that his scientific ghost hunt had led him to a woman who tried to kill him with a fork, like a witch in a fairy tale! That evening he lost another chess game to his colleague Rageet, who seemed amused by the evidence of a female's physical superiority.

Just after writing these last few lines, I received a call from my son, Randolph, in Boston; he's a pediatrician too, you'll remember. He is the father of two

152

sons—Peter, who's seven, and Ronnie, five. A third's on the way, a girl, I hope. Randolph, who doesn't like to talk about my illness, tried to cheer me up with a story about his sons. They'd been playing with plastic figurines, some of which were pirates, and a fierce quarrel had developed between them. The younger one, Ronnie, believed all pirates are bad, and tried to prove it conclusively by pointing out that almost every pirate had a black eye patch, a hook, or a wooden leg; so obviously they were all evil. Peter, who's slightly older, was upset. *All* pirates aren't bad, he insisted, there are good ones too. For three days the boys refused to talk to each other, and finally my son tried to mediate: pirates are basically robbers, he said, and robbers are bad, but there are some who are good and kind who steal from the rich and give to the poor, like Robin Hood. "They haven't made up yet," Randolph told me, "but at least they're talking." I was glad; I laughed. Once a grandpa, always a grandpa.

Shortly before going to sleep I remembered a story about two famous leaders during the Reformation. They were arguing about transubstantiation. One of them insisted that the sacrament actually and literally transformed the bread and wine into Christ's body; the other man maintained that the whole thing had to be taken symbolically. "That's how it is," shouted the first. "That's how it seems," shouted the other, and they separated. A religious war. To arms! How much more sophisticated my grandsons are, at least when it comes to deciding whether a pirate's a bad guy or not.

I had a good night's sleep.

40

Mary of course immediately hurried home to Chris Cramer, who by this time had moved to a squalid room in a Third Avenue rooming house at Thirty-third Street, right under the elevated tracks. Chris Cramer helped her pack her clothes and utensils and asked no questions. She gave him an address where he could find her, and hid her hair and forehead under a scarf, as if her mug shot had already been pinned up in every police station. She hugged Chris Cramer and ran away.

In response to my grandfather's rather gloating amusement over his colleague's escape from the lady with the fork, Soper had offered a bet: that he would be able to enter Mary's house without any weapon and without a police escort. An uncanny feeling overcame him, though, when a tall, thin, middle-aged man opened the door, looked at him with an almost dreamy expression in his eyes, and asked whether he was a doctor.

And how did he know, asked Soper.

It smells that way, answered Chris Cramer. He invited Soper in, chasing away two cats that lay curled up together on a chair. The room smelled of vegetables and cat piss and was altogether badly ventilated, and when Soper noticed a rat that seemed not only unperturbed by the cats but keenly interested in him, he was afraid. Nevertheless, he tried to concentrate.

Chris Cramer observed him silently, but not without friendliness. "You seem to be a passionate reader," Soper remarked after a glance at all the books strewn about the room.

Chris Cramer nodded and inconspicuously placed an open pamphlet so that it covered an alarm clock and small spool of wire. Shakespeare, Dickens, and Twain, he answered, immediately winning the doctor's heart. After a long conversation about *David Copperfield*, Soper finally plucked up the courage to ask about Mary Mallon. Did he know her? Chris Cramer nodded. Soper told Chris Cramer of his suspicion: that Mary was a carrier of a disease to which she herself was immune. He searched carefully for the right words. A German bacteriologist had discovered the phenomenon a few years ago, he said. It didn't make Mary criminal, he added; far from it. She could be helped with medication; at the very worst it might require minor surgery of the gallbladder.

Chris Cramer interrupted him. "Come back in three days," he said, "and make sure you come alone. No cops."

When Soper came back three days later he received a promise that Mary would be waiting for him there at nine o'clock sharp the next morning. Soper did not for a moment consider giving Mary a chance to escape. Undercover policemen were patrolling the area by eight in the morning, much to the amusement of the neighborhood, since anyone could spot a policeman play-acting.

Soper knocked on the door and called: "Miss Mallon! Miss Mallon! It's me, Dr. Soper, a friend!" Finally he stepped in. Mary stood in the middle of the room, lips pressed together, hands clasped behind her back. Soper was not ashamed to repeat the phrase with which Stanley had made a fool of himself in front of Livingston: "Miss Mallon, I presume?" Mary did not answer, so he continued: "Mary, I've come to talk to you. You say you have never caused a case of typhoid, but I know you have done so. Nobody thinks you have done it purposely. When you go to the toilet, the germs which grow within your body get upon your fingers. And if after that—just to use an example—you touch some lettuce, these germs—I mean, if, for example, you washed your hands every time—"

He got no further than that. In his embarrassment he had again expressed himself badly; at any rate, Mary's right hand held a knife pointed at him, a butcher's knife. Slowly she followed the retreating, blanching Dr. Soper. "You shameless son of a bitch," she whispered, and stepped closer.

Soper pulled out his police whistle, but before he could put it to his lips, two men dashed into the room, effortlessly subdued Mary, and dragged her downstairs.

And once again he'd played the fool, as he confessed to his colleague in a propitiously friendly moment: the two men had not been policemen, but neighbors of Chris Cramer, who was always gentle as a dove and wise as a serpent.

41

Dr. George A. Soper was worn out. Not that his inquisitive scientist's mind had grown tired, but he was tired of playing cops and robbers, and the prospect of becoming a cartoon character in the New York dailies did not appeal to him, either. Needless to say, the police covered up this last mishap. He sent a letter informing the city's Board of Health that the escaped Mary Mallon represented a "public menace"; and since Mary was considered a myth by the Board of Health, he did not forget to mention a statistic according to which approximately twenty-three thousand Americans had fallen prey to typhoid in the previous year. Sooner or later, he concluded, Mary Mallon might precipitate a major epidemic in New York. The Board of Health commissioned an inspector, Dr. S. Josephine

Baker, to pursue the case of Mary Mallon. Was it a challenge to the authorities or an act of naïve self-confidence that had made Mary return to Chris Cramer's rooming house just a few hours after the bungled arrest?

She showed no sign of surprise when Dr. Josephine Baker (that was really her name) knocked on the door and asked her to voluntarily submit to a physical examination. According to Dr. Baker, Mary fixed her with glittering eyes and rage-contorted features and told her to go to hell. And so Dr. Baker returned that same day, March 4, with an ambulance, three policemen, and a warrant for Mary Mallon's arrest.

Mary had disappeared, and so had Chris Cramer. Dr. Baker had the three policemen search the house, instructing them to not just turn over the mattress and bed but also to tip over the wardrobe, as if Mary might conceivably have turned into a mouse. One policeman went so far as to beat up a laundry basket with his nightstick, without success. A search conducted in the neighboring rooms was equally unsuccessful. Dr. Baker was about to throw in the towel when one of the policemen discovered a wardrobe with a muslin curtain hidden behind a barricade of garbage pails at the far end of a hallway. That was where she was.

With a mighty cat's leap Mary flung herself at the policemen who came running to help their colleague. She knocked the hats off their heads, shrieked and cursed, bit them and clawed at their eyes, kicked one man's chin with a heel, dented another's front teeth with a knee, and tore a piece of one policeman's ear off as if it were made of paper. The police had expected a modest struggle; instead they found themselves in something close to a massacre. Blood spattered clothes, floor, and walls. (Twenty years later, one cop wrote in his memoirs that a kick in his manhood had rendered him

159

unfit to father a fourth child he had wished for.) Mary fought, screamed like a mothering sow whose suckling piglets are being torn from her teats, moaned, howled, and lamented miserably until the men managed to stuff her mouth with cloth, handcuff her hands behind her back, and bind her legs with leather belts. Since the people in this part of town were not particularly fond of the police, it wasn't long before bottles and bricks came flying out of the windows. Another proof of Mary's popularity.

"I sat next to her in the ambulance," writes Dr. Baker. "It was like being locked up in a cage with a lioness."

Mary was brought to a cell with whitewashed walls and bars—a hospital, not a prison: the Williard Parker Hospital for infectious diseases. She demanded to know what they wanted of her. Nothing much: just a sample of her urine, her stool, and her blood. The doctor examining her was a gaunt elderly man who watched her with cold detached eyes, as if she were a guinea pig being prepared for vivisection. The nurses had untied Mary's hands and legs, dressed her in a long hospital shift, and then strapped her to a wooden bench with a pot underneath. For two days she sat in despair and confusion on this throne of degradation. Her bowels were cramped, and she let out a cry of pain when the petrified stool left her intestine.

42

After the examination, Mary was transported to Riverside Hospital on North Brother Island. She was not treated badly. She lived in a tiny bungalow originally intended for the head nurse. It had a bedroom, a bathroom, and a kitchen with a gas stove and an electric light bulb in the ceiling. Each room had a view across the water to the shore. There was even a church around the corner. No iron bars, though in the evening the front door was locked from the outside. Soper had told the hospital administrators Mary was a passionate cook; they had meat and vegetables delivered to her bungalow so she could prepare her own meals. She was alone and isolated, but every Tuesday and Friday she was allowed to go to the library and take books home in the company of a nurse. When the doctor came for her daily checkup, she asked only one question: "When can I leave?" and answered none herself. Several times Soper tried to convince her she was in fact healthy, although her health was a kind of sickness; her answer was always: "No!" He sent her books, wrote simply worded treatises about her peculiar typhoid disease. Always just: "No!"

Every criminal has a right to legal counsel. Not Mary. The courts and the Board of Health tripped over one another's red tape. Files gathered dust. Chris Cramer's letters were full of love, though he never used the word; nor did he write about himself. One thing she couldn't understand was that he never asked any questions about her "case," though she knew he must have his reasons. He told her of the death of one of their two cats, run over by a cart; of new buildings called skyscrapers; of snow that had piled up so high all traffic had been stopped for two days and hundreds of people had frozen to death in the slums. During the summer he wrote with childlike pride about an electric ventilator he had bought, a new invention that made hot nights more bearable.

She began to suffer from insomnia and horrific daydreams. She was on the *Leibnitz* again, nursing her dying parents and sisters. She had never talked about them, never thought about them in all those years; they had never even appeared in her dreams before. Sean Mallon the cook was there, too. He could knock a fifty-pound flour sack off the top of a table with a single punch of his fist and make it come down right side up without tipping over. Once one of the sacks split open, and for several minutes, to Mary's enormous delight, the ship's kitchen was filled with clouds of flour dust. Sometimes he would sit her down on top of the table and feel her all over; this he called "kneading the dough." Her parents' and sisters' corpses had gone overboard long ago, without a prayer, without a word. A few days later she had thrown her little sister's doll into the sea so she'd have something to play with. The captain lay sick in his cabin, unable to flag a warning that there was an epidemic on board. Mary spent the whole day in the kitchen helping Sean Mallon cook for the crew. Sometimes she'd bring a few plates with leftovers down to the orlop. Sean Mallon adopted her as his daughter. "I'll teach you how to cook," he said, "and once we're in New York we'll leave this floating coffin. There's millions of Irish swarming about there, and you and me, we'll open a restaurant."

Then, after a few days, his walk became unsteady. He started cursing and cutting his fingers while he worked. He shook his head as if trying to shake the dizziness out of it, and sank to his knees. There was a saying at the time: An Irishman never kneels. But down he went on his knees nonetheless, then fell onto his stomach, hammering the floor with his feet. Blood flowed from his nose; his eyes were staring. Now, many years later, he sat by Mary's bedside and consoled her. Sometimes children from her village back home, from Rhäzüns, would sit there too, talking in dialect and singing. The doctors put her to sleep with pills. The next night, hailstones the size of pigeon's eggs fell on the roof. She sat up, alert as a blackbird, counting the rattling blows as fast as she could. She was convinced she hadn't missed a single hailstone and concluded she must be in her right mind after all.

The next day a young lawyer knocked on her door; his name was George Francis O'Neill. He held out his hand—an unexpected gesture, both for its courteousness and for its disregard of her condition—and told her that so far every lawyer had refused to take on her case.

The young lawyer made no bones about his own ambition. He explained to Mary that her incarceration was unconstitutional, since no charges had been brought against her. "All they have on you," he said, "is a bunch of official files without any legal meaning whatsoever."

Fourteen days later, Mary appeared in court and swore that she had never had typhoid and therefore couldn't have infected anyone. A doctor (not George A. Soper, curiously) took the stand as expert witness and asserted, against all of Mary's declarations, that the presence of typhus bacilli in Mary's stool had been proven beyond all reasonable doubt. No doubt he was right about that. But the court was still violating the Constitution, as the young lawyer demonstrated. Nevertheless, Mary had to return to isolation for three years, until the Board of Health, reluctantly and with a guilty conscience, decided to "pardon" her until further notice. Mary had to sign an official promise not to engage in any kind of cooking, or in any work involving the handling of food or food products. In addition, she was to report to the Board of Health every three weeks. O'Neill had won. Mary thanked him and the Board of Health, was set free, and disappeared.

She broke her promise immediately, made up one alias after another, cooked—as an assistant—in restaurants and hotels, then again in elegant households. Strangely, no one ever suspected her. Not once. Mary's public image remained faceless. She had aged. Here and there cases of typhoid broke out, the newspapers quipped, and whenever someone died who wasn't particularly well liked, people would whisper that the deceased had had his eggs scrambled by Typhoid Mary.

For a while the beautiful name "Mary" fell into disrepute. From time to time in fancy restaurants a customer amused himself by spoiling some diner's appetite with the casual remark that the cook's name was Mary.

As for the real Mary, no one believed in her.

43

The world was not very kind
to Mary," writes Soper. A genteel understatement if
there ever was one. Mary switched jobs as often as she
moved, usually from one dirty, unfriendly lodging house
to another. Chris Cramer, who usually stayed at home
reading, was turning into a recluse, sour and grumpy,
only rarely seeing friends. But whenever Mary came to
visit, he would brighten up. He had never said a word
about her "sickness," just as he had never told her
anything about himself. He talked about neighbors,
about new books and writers he had discovered; there
were times when he'd spend a whole evening telling
Mary what had happened in this or that book, and
reading the most successful passages out loud. He was
such a good storyteller that Mary was usually disap-

pointed when she read the book herself. Since he never cooked for himself and generally ate very little, Mary would always make sure to cook something he could heat up for himself for a few days, usually a soup or stew; and it was not by mutual agreement that she put a couple of dollars in his coat pocket every time she dropped in for a visit. He seemed not to need any money at all. Mary was proud of having always stood by a man who had no ambition and whose presumed innocence she loved.

The end came suddenly. One evening she no longer found him at home. She waited until two in the morning, then turned off the ventilator, the only device in his room (aside from the light bulb) indicative of the new century. Morning came, and he hadn't come home. She waited till noon, then, without a moment's hesitation, walked into the local police station. She knew there was no warrant for her arrest, but that wouldn't have scared her away in any case. The officer on duty took down a few notes and told Mary to come back in the early afternoon. At three o'clock she learned the awful news. Chris Cramer had collapsed in the street; his body was in the morgue. Someone had to go and immediately identify him.

"By the shore of the East River, below 26th Street, stands a massive gray building known as Bellevue Hospital," it says in the old New York guidebook before me, and a little further on: "Above a basement door, beneath the steps leading up to the entrance, is a sign bearing a single word in gilded letters: MORGUE."

Mary got into a whispering match with an official because she couldn't prove she was a relative. She lied by the Bible and all the saints and secretly slipped ten dollars into the man's hand. He nodded, went away, and took a half hour to come back, then led her through narrow passages into a room where five corpses lay covered with sheets. The official lifted the sheet off one of the bodies, uncovering head and chest. A stranger. Mary shook her head, to the official's obvious annoyance. Then, with four quick tugs and without batting an eyelash, he pulled the sheets off the other bodies and walked out. The body of the man in the middle was the one Chris Cramer had lived in. She kissed his forehead with her eyes closed, and genuflected. Then she took a sheet of paper out of her pocketbook, folded it several times, and hid it beneath his folded hands. She covered him up again. After a silent moment, she covered the other bodies as well.

She walked out unnoticed, for others had arrived in the waiting room.

44

Mary returned to his room on Third Avenue and began to pack his belongings into boxes. But where to put it all? Where to leave the books he loved so much? Chris Cramer had never talked about his family, just as Mary had always avoided mentioning hers. She knew his handful of friends by first name only, and in recent years he hadn't talked about them either.

Chris Cramer's body was taken to Potter's Field, laid in a heap with other unclaimed bodies, and covered with two dozen shovelfuls of earth. Aside from Mary's letters, there remained no sign, no evidence of his existence; no official papers, no passport. It was as if he had never lived in the city, but only for Mary, and for his ideas and books. Nothing else.

Nothing? Thanks to her thoroughness, Mary found a dusty folder tied with string, which contained articles and reports about an event that had shaken the whole country years ago. After reading the innumerable articles, Mary realized that Chris Cramer had not been merely a strange bird, a perpetual outsider, but one of the most wanted men in America. Since the early 1880s Chris Cramer had been a member of an anarchist movement. In 1886 he had been in Chicago at the so-called Haymarket Square riot, a demonstration of workers that began peacefully and ended with a mass rally on the haymarket, where leaflets by the German anarchist August Spies were being distributed. Sometime after two hundred policemen had appeared from all sides and surrounded the square, someone suddenly threw a handmade bomb into a group of policemen. It exploded, killing several policemen and wounding some bystanders. Two men clearly implicated were punished with life sentences. The alleged leaders were sentenced to death and hanged. One man, however, was known to have escaped—the one who had thrown the bomb: Chris Cramer.

Mary felt proud and sad at the same time. He had not been lonely by choice after all. His melancholy came from feelings of guilt. If he had turned himself in, every one of the defendants would have been sentenced to death, including the ones who got away with life sentences. So it wasn't cowardice. Eventually he was able to convince his anarchist comrades that they would be in danger if he continued working with them. He would probably be tortured if he was caught, and he was no hero: they could see that for themselves by the miserably shaky manner in which he had thrown that bomb. From now on he would send

170

the families of the *murdered* policemen every dollar he could spare.

All this could be gleaned from comments scribbled in the margins of the newspaper articles. Among the marginal notes was the following remark: "Either every human being is guilty of what he does; or, on the contrary: everyone is innocent, despite everything he has done. I can't decide. May I be forgiven. Chris Cramer."

Mary wept.

I, Howard J. Rageet, M.D., am inclined to agree with Chris Cramer's statement: I am neither for nor against euthanasia. I am on the side of the doctor who refuses to administer the *coup de grâce*, and equally on the side of the dying patient who demands his death.

Yesterday I read in the newspaper that in Western Europe a company named Unicer Holding, an enormously profitable waste-disposal business, had dumped seventy-two thousand tons of poisonous chemical refuse, "without a trace," in the middle of a forest in order to save time and money. How many people—no, how many children—will die as a consequence? A gentleman's misdemeanor. No doubt the courts will come up with some mitigating circumstances.

In a few years the death penalty will be reintroduced everywhere with such matter-of-factness that neither its advocates nor its opponents will have any time to argue about it. It will be carried out without any change in the laws.

Ten minutes ago Lea called to ask how I was feeling. This weekend, she says, she would like to introduce me to her future husband. I'd love to meet him, I replied. Is he a doctor? She said yes. "Thank God for that," I said, and Lea laughed. "Good night," she said, "good night, Dad."

Now I've given myself an injection and have sat down to watch the late movie with Humphrey Bogart, another doctor's son, good Lord.

45

I've been feeling better today, quite amazingly better. In my condition, that's almost certainly a bad sign.

Why, after Chris Cramer's death, did she work as a cook in a children's hospital? After all, she loved children. Sometimes people will turn in self-hate against what they love most. It's possible, though, that she wanted to prove something: Look, I worked for two months in a children's hospital. Not a single child died of typhoid fever, not one. (I ask myself now as a doctor whether the virulence of her carrier disease might not have diminished by then.) Or was she looking for the child she had lost? A child that would resemble Chris Cramer?

Or was it just a failed attempt at revenge? Fate had taught her to be cold-blooded. After two months in the children's hospital she quit her job. Nothing had happened.

Two weeks later Mary took a position as a cook in a women's hospital, and another two weeks later a Dr. Edward Cragin called Dr. George Soper, urging him to come to Cragin's office immediately. Cragin was a gynecologist at Sloane's Hospital. More than twenty patients had contracted typhus. There was a middle-aged lady, one of the kitchen personnel, who he suspected could be the ghost everyone was talking about. The possibility had dawned on him when he heard some of the staff cracking jokes about there being a Typhoid Mary among them, and when he noticed this particular woman laughing out loud at the mention of the name, he felt almost certain. She had just left the building, and wouldn't be back till evening. "Do you think you would recognize her handwriting after all these years?" he asked. "I don't want to needlessly hurt this woman's feelings, she's popular here, and she seems rather sad . . ."

A half hour later, Soper arrived at Cragin's office and immediately recognized the handwriting. The piece of paper Cragin had handed him was a letter signed "Mrs. Helen Gordon." It was an application for a job as hospital cook. Soper notified the Board of Health and asked for assistance.

That evening, shortly before eight, Mary was seized by three plainclothes officers. They wrapped her up in blankets and packed her away in a car. It took only seconds, and no one but a couple of passersby stopped to watch. She had put up no resistance. She ended up on North Brother Island in the same bungalow she had lived in five years earlier.

Mary did not try to flee, and would not answer questions either. During interrogations she watched flies, flies invisible to all but her. Once a reporter came to ask

174

questions about her love life. She threw him out, and not just with words. Gradually, according to the hospital records, she became reasonable, and returned to the bosom of the Church. Still, she refused to pray, despite long discussions with the hospital priest. She *couldn't* pray, she said once. Others would have to do that for her. After two years, she was finally given permission to go shopping or visiting in Manhattan once every three weeks. But there was no one in Manhattan she could have visited.

Some twilight thoughts. Was it Chris Cramer's death, was it loneliness, an irrevocable, inescapable loneliness, or was it flight from loneliness that made her choose to play the role of an avenging angel? Or did she want to avenge her own fate? What thoughts might occur to an uneducated woman made to realize that she brings death to others but cannot choose her victims? What I imagine is this: nothing but a huge indifference. The indifference that attacks us all occasionally, and that is now breaking in upon us as the latest and probably the final spiritual plague.

A specter is haunting the world: the specter of hopelessness.

Three A.M. It was not the pain that woke me up, it was my conscience, barking into my sleep with bare fangs like a pack of wolves. The ghost of hopelessness is *my* ghost; I have no right to bequeath it to my descendants.

Another thing that woke me was a burst of noise in this usually quiet and anonymous house, the sound of raucous singing from an open window two or three floors above me: "Happy birthday to you . . ." In my sleep it sounded like a mockery.

When my wife died, I mourned; I was desperate, even though I never loved her. And I'm well aware of the fact that by saying this I am not violating any oath of confidentiality, but am merely confessing to myself.

Tomorrow I'll try to describe Mary's motives—no, not the motives, there aren't any. But maybe I'll be able to imagine something.

My imagination is growing dim. I don't need it anymore.

To whom it may concern:

I, Lea Sandra Rageet, am concluding these chapters from the life of Mary Mallon alias Typhoid Mary. My father passed away eight days ago—by his own choice.

The notes I found lying in a small folder next to the manuscript can be summed up in a few sentences. My father's sharp, resolute handwriting deteriorated rapidly on the last pages, each letter standing out separately like a chiseled vignette, but there is a clearly legible reference to my great-grandfather's calendar, underlined in red. I leafed through the calendar, and to my surprise I found several descriptions of visits he paid Mary on North Brother Island. She seems to have gotten along well with him—much better than with Dr. Soper, whom she never forgave. The reason may be that the Rageet family originally came from Graubünden, where she was born. Apparently as she got older Mary no longer insisted—other than ironically—on Sean Mallon being recognized as her father. She had become "droll and pious" in her old age, according to my great-grandfather, and she could remember her early childhood with astonishing accuracy. She had a recollection, for instance, of the village pastor, a man named Fopp, handing a ridiculous sum of money to the impoverished family father Caduff on the day of his departure for America, a sort of earnest from Mother Church. The purest hypocrisy: the community wanted to get rid of the family, since they were afraid the Caduffs might end up living off the parish.

But Mary, who spoke of her later life as a "closed incident," had to endure another ordeal which as a doctor even I'm tempted to call diabolical. One summer evening in 1930 a nurse found her lying on the floor of her bungalow (fellow patients often came to visit, and left during Mary's mealtimes). She was almost immobile, one eyelid half closed, her arms and legs stretched out. The diagnosis: brain hemorrhage. She

178

could no longer speak, only moan, and had to be spoon-fed from then on. For eight long years she lived in this fashion.

She died on November 11, 1938—as my father mentioned at the beginning of the book—and was taken to a cemetery and buried that same day. The following morning there was a service at St. Luke's Church on 138th Street in the Bronx. Nine people knelt and prayed in the front row; none identified himself to the priest. And no one seemed interested in the few pewter plates and silver candleholders she left behind either, nor did anyone claim her money, which wasn't much but nothing to scoff at—a few hundred dollars after all.

Lea S. Rageet
Boston, Fall 1981.

P.S. Among my father's notes was a document, yellowed and worn by frequent handling, signed by Mary: presumably a present from Mrs. Julia Seeley, the pleasant lady who brought Mary and some of her victims together. She is said to have visited Mary occasionally before her stroke, and perhaps Mary passed it on to my great-grandfather. Here it is:

Mr. W. K. Vanderbilt

MENU

Huîtres

POTAGES

Consommé Rachel   Bisque d'écrevisses

HORS-D'OEUVRE

Timbales napolitaines

RELEVÉS

Escalopes de bass, Henri IV   Pommes de terre
surprise
Selle de mouton Salvandi

ENTREES

Caisses de filets de grouses Grammont
Choux de Bruxelles   Petits pois à l'anglaise
Sauté de filets de grouses tyrolienne

Celeri au jus

—————

Sorbet Aya Pana

—————

RÔTIS

Canvasback duck   Cailles trufflées
Salade de laitue

ENTREMETS SUCRÉS

Pudding à la Humboldt
Gelée d'orange orientale   Gaufres à la creme
Blancmange rubane   Charlotte Victoria
Glaces fruits-en-surprise   Delicious Impèriale

ABOUT THE ILLUSTRATOR

LARRY SCHWINGER attended the Philadelphia College of Art, the training ground of a long line of American artists beginning with Thomas Eakins. From a job as a courtroom artist, he moved into advertising and projects for the Broadway theatre, before making a deep artistic commitment to mass market publishing. His paintings cover an enormous spectrum of techniques and subject matter, exemplifying the best in contemporary American illustration. Schwinger lives in New Jersey with his son in a 100-year-old farmhouse.